THE
PETRELLI HEIR

THE
PETRELLI HEIR

BY

KIM LAWRENCE

First published in Great Britain 2013
by Mills & Boon, an imprint of Harlequin (UK) Limited.
Large Print edition 2013
Harlequin (UK) Limited, Eton House,
18-24 Paradise Road, Richmond, Surrey TW9 1SR

© Kim Lawrence 2013

ISBN: 978 0 263 23184 7

Harlequin (UK) policy is to use papers that are natural,
renewable and recyclable products and made from
wood grown in sustainable forests. The logging and
manufacturing process conform to the legal environmental
regulations of the country of origin.

Printed and bound in Great Britain
by CPI Antony Rowe, Chippenham, Wiltshire

PROLOGUE

London
June 2010

IZZY let out a startled yelp as her heel caught
in a hole in the pavement and brought her to an
abrupt stumbling halt. Wincing, she flexed her
narrow ankle experimentally. Fortunately it held
her weight when she put it back down again.

No damage but her feet hurt.

Why?

It took her a few moments to connect the ache
in her feet with the time she'd been walking. She
glanced at her watch, scrunching her eyes to read
the face concealed by the cuff of her thin jacket.
What time had she started walking?

Her smooth brow furrowed as she tried to sort
out the confused sequence of the day's events in
her head. It had been afternoon when she had

shaken the hand of her mother's solicitor and thanked the funeral director. There had been no one else to thank, no one else to exchange amusing anecdotes of the departed with.

Her mother, Dr Ruth Carter, famous in the academic world all her professional life and famous outside it since her one attempt at a populist book landed her with an international best-seller that had broken all previous records for a non-fiction book.

The royalty cheques still kept dropping on the doormat—Izzy's doormat now. She was almost rich… Was that a bit like being nearly famous…? Izzy shook her head. For no reason at all she suddenly wanted to laugh or was that cry? No, not cry, she didn't think she had any more tears available to shed. They were all frozen in the lead weight that lay hard and heavy pressing against her breastbone.

Dr Ruth Carter had enjoyed her fame as a celebrity psychologist, and had become a firm favourite on breakfast television shows. There were probably many people who would have liked to come and pay their last respects, but Ruth Carter had had firm views about funerals.

No religion.

No fuss or flowers.

No wake.

No fuss and no tears.

Her only child, actually her only living relative, Izzy had respected her wishes and she hadn't cried. She hadn't even cried when she had found her mother's body and the neat handwritten note, written as she spoke in that distinctive bullet-point dogmatic style.

In the weeks that followed both the police and then coroner at the inquest had praised her composure and bravery, but Izzy hadn't been brave. She had been numb, and now, today, she was… angry, she realised, identifying the emotion that was making her chest tight. She had kept walking because she was afraid that if she stopped all that anger would spill out and she had a mental image of herself enveloped in an angry toxic cloud.

She wasn't angry with her mother for choosing the time and manner in which she died. The insidious terminal disease that had slowly been robbing her mother of her ability to function independently, keeping her locked in a helpless body, had been terrible. No, her mother had made her choice in her time, the note had said.

And to hell with everyone else!

Her mother hadn't said that, but during the clinical goodbye today Izzy had thought it. So, yes, she was angry! The doctors had said her mother had at least another twelve months of relatively normal life, months when Izzy could have said all the things she would never say now.

Not even goodbye.

And now today her mother had reached out from the grave and… Izzy unfolded her stiff fingers from the typed letter that lay scrunched in her pocket and lifted a hand to her head. The dampness on her skin and her hair came as a surprise and she stared at the wet shiny pavement. She hadn't even realised it had been raining.

She didn't even know where she was! Or for that matter who she was…? She knew she wasn't the product of a contribution by an anonymous sperm donor.

It turned out she had a *real* father, one who was right now receiving a similar letter to the one the solicitor had handed her this afternoon. Apparently, the poor man had been an eighteen-year-old student at the time, selected as a suitable genetic father and seduced by her forty-something mother, who had been reacting to her ticking body clock.

Why had her mother lied?

Why had she told her now?

Why had she left her alone?

Izzy straightened her slender shoulders and gave herself a strong talking to. *Focus! You can't fall apart, you're capable—everyone says it, so surely it must be true.*

Where are you, capable Izzy?

As she looked vaguely around a door opened to a nearby building and sounds of people talking and laughing spilled out, all so normal…how weird.

Without meaning to she followed the sound and

found herself in a bar. She loosened the button on her jacket, aware that she was thirsty. It was warm and humid and crowded as she began to work her way through several groups of people standing; all the tables were full, except one.

Izzy's restless gaze was drawn as if by some invisible magnet to that table or, more specifically, to the man who sat at it.

He was the most beautiful man she had ever seen!

The sheer awfulness of the day fell away and she stood stock still, oblivious to the curious stares she drew. As she stared at the man her heart hammered against her ribcage, her throat became dry and her knees were quite literally shaking, but not with exhaustion. She no longer felt weary but energised, her body taut and tingling with a squirmy, stomach-clenching excitement.

The man put down his drink and stared back, dragging his dark hair from his wide bronzed brow. Izzy shivered, as if the man had touched her, which was crazy, and she pressed a hand to her stomach where the fluid heat was spreading outwards.

On a purely aesthetic level he was someone people would always stare at. His face could have belonged to a classical statue and was a miracle of classical symmetry. He had incredible carved cheekbones, an aquiline nose and sculpted lips that were both sensual and cruel…?

Izzy shivered again. Just then a group of noisy, slightly the worse for wear young men bumped into her, the physical jolt wrenching her from the bold, overtly sexual scrutiny of those dark eyes. She turned her head sharply and thought, *My God, I'm panting!*

A man had never looked at her that way—as if he wanted her—or if one had Izzy hadn't noticed. Not enough to do anything about it anyhow. Not a sexual creature, Izzy's mother had proclaimed— her professional opinion—after first ruling out the possibility her daughter was actually gay, but in denial about her sexuality.

My mum, the big fan of plain speaking; my mum, who respected honesty; oh, yes, my pain-

fully honest mum. Izzy felt the letter again—the bombshell honest Dr Carter had exploded when she was no longer around to answer for the biggest lie of them all—and felt her anger rise up once more. Well, maybe she could, just for once, prove her mother wrong?

Just because she'd never experienced blinding lust before didn't mean Izzy didn't recognise it when she felt it. She dabbed her tongue to the moisture that had broken out along her upper lip, still staring at the man even with a solid wall of people between her and those dark disturbing eyes.

The crowd of men jostled her again, moving in close and delivering a few good-natured comments that Izzy didn't even register. As she approached the bar she was still seeing those dark hungry eyes. She focused on them—it wasn't hard—and seeing them, feeling them, she didn't have to think about anything else.

'Are you eighteen?' the barman asked for the third time, studying the young woman's glazed blue eyes and wondering if she was on something.

'No, yes…I mean, I'm twenty-one…almost.'

Izzy was not surprised when he asked, 'You got some identity, miss?'

Flustered, she reached into her bag and found her driving licence, holding her thick wavy chestnut hair back from her face with her forearm when it flopped in her eyes.

The barman raised his brows as he scanned it before producing her drink and an apologetic, 'We have to check.'

She jumped when a beefy, slightly clammy hand landed on top of her own, pressing it into the surface of the bar. 'A beautiful woman should never pay for her own drink,' the owner of the hand slurred.

Oh, God, and the hits just kept coming, she thought, her nostrils flaring in distaste as she inhaled the beer-laden fumes of her admirer.

'Thank you, but I'm meeting someone…excuse me.'

The man didn't move. If anything, egged on

by his mates, he moved in closer. Izzy hunched in on herself defensively.

Not a violent or angry person, diplomatic Izzy balled her hand into a fist in her head. She could hear her mother saying, *When you have to shout, Izzy, you have lost an argument.*

But her mum wasn't here.

'Go away, you creep!'

I just yelled, and it felt good.

'*Cara*, I'm sorry I'm late but...' The men crowding around her suddenly parted to reveal the unbelievably attractive lone wolf from the table. Lean and broad-shouldered, all hard muscle and sinew, he was a head taller than the drunk pestering her and he had the entire mean, brooding hungry look going on, boosted by the combustible gleam in his narrowed eyes.

Izzy couldn't tear her gaze away from his face and she wanted to touch him so much it hurt, which was crazy. She was gazing with helpless admiration at the long curling ebony lashes that framed those spectacular eyes when with zero warning he fitted his mouth to hers as though he'd done it a hundred times before and kissed her hard, full on the mouth.

It was only when he lifted his mouth that he even appeared to notice the other men.

'Is there a problem?' No longer languid and warm, his deep voice was layered with icy hauteur.

Problem? she thought, swallowing a bubble of hysteria. Did standing there staring or not being able to breathe count? His kiss had tasted of whisky, she thought as she ran her tongue across the outline of her own trembling mouth. The younger men almost fell over themselves to assure the stranger that there was no problem at all as they vanished like mist.

'You looked like you were about to deck him. You're a feisty little thing, aren't you?'

Izzy unclenched her fist. 'That was very resourceful of you, but I didn't need saving.' *I'm feisty!*

This close, the raw maleness that had given her a hormone rush from across the room was a million times more intense.

'No…?' His shoulders lifted in an expressive shrug as he stared at her, dragging his hand back and forth across the dark stubble shadowing his square jaw. His eyes slid to the glass in her hand. 'You were planning to drown your sorrows?' His mouth curled into a self-derisive sneer as he added softly, 'Stare into the bottom of a glass and feel sorry for yourself?'

Izzy looked at the glass in her hand… Was she?

'I wish you more luck than me.'

Was he saying he was drunk? He didn't look drunk. He didn't sound drunk. In fact his rich, gravelly, slightly accented voice was delicious— he was delicious.

Her heart raced; the sexual tension between them was like a wall cutting them off from the rest of the room. The reckless exhilaration fizzing through her bloodstream made her feel dizzy.

'I don't want a drink any more,' Izzy said breathlessly, at the same time wondering what she was doing.

Whatever it was it felt good.

His dark eyes didn't leave hers for a moment.

'You don't? What do you want?' His brow furrowed. 'How remiss of me. I'm—'

'No!' Izzy reached up and pressed a warning finger to his lips. Once there she found herself tracing the firm outline, fascinated by the texture and warmth of his skin. 'I don't need to know your name. I need—'

He caught her hand and held it by his face and slurred throatily, 'What do you need, *cara*?' His thumb stroked a line down her cheek as he bent in close and whispered, 'Tell me...'

His gravelly accented drawl made her insides dissolve.

'I've had a very bad day and I don't want to think about it. I need...' She paused. Life-changing revelations or not, twenty years of sensible caution did not give up without a fight. The man could be a homicidal maniac...he could...he could...he could...

Izzy closed her eyes and opened them again. She needed not to think, she needed to feel...his skin. Desire washed over her like a flash fire, dragging the breath from her lungs and making her skin prickle.

'I think I need you.' *Is this really me saying that?*

'Think?'

'I need you.'

It was definitely her leaving a bar with an enigmatic, beautiful stranger.

CHAPTER ONE

Izzy hurried up the aisle, her heels clicking on the marble floor as she went. She pretended to be unaware of the scattering of nudges and not so discreet whispered comments that followed her progress. She pretended extremely well—she'd had practice.

It would have been nice to think people were riveted by her stunning fashion sense, but the reality was that, while the misty blue silk chiffon dress did bring out the blue in her blue-grey eyes and made her rich chestnut hair look more auburn than brown, it was a little too snug across her post-baby bust. And besides, the church was filled with a lot of women who were better dressed and, in her opinion, better looking—short and skinny with freckles was an acquired taste.

But the attention she garnered had nothing to do with the way she looked and everything to do with her being there at all, because everyone there knew that Izzy was not a real Fitzgerald!

Two years ago when Izzy had first arrived in the small Cumbrian market town, her appearance had attracted much more attention, but happily she was yesterday's news. The pregnant illegitimate daughter that Michael Fitzgerald had not known he had was a scandal still, but no longer one that was likely to steal the show. And things were improving.

Izzy's expression softened as her thoughts caused her glance to drift to where her father sat talking to his brother, the father of the bride. The two men with their leonine heads of grey-streaked strawberry-blond hair were alike enough to have passed for twins, though Jake Fitzgerald was older by three years.

As if feeling her gaze Michael turned his head and winked at her and Izzy grinned back. Her father was a remarkable man. How many men receiving a letter telling them that they had a daughter from an affair twenty years ago would have reacted the way he had?

Not many, she suspected. But Michael hadn't even wanted the DNA test! In fact the entire family had been great and instead of treating her like a cuckoo in the nest they had opened their collective arms and drawn her into the protective inner family circle.

She had been a stranger to these people, yet when she had been at her most vulnerable they had been there for her. After a lifetime of believing it was a weakness to rely on other people Izzy had initially found it difficult to accept their help, but their warmth had thawed her natural diffidence. Asking for help was still not her first instinct, in fact she hated it, but she was learning that sometimes there was no choice but to grit your teeth and swallow your pride. A lot of things changed when you had a baby.

Izzy's attention suddenly turned to her auburn-headed young half-brother, handsome in his morning suit and deep in conversation with someone sitting next to the aisle in the row behind. He really needed to take his seat. 'Rory, come on. She's here.'

Rory straightened up with a grin. 'Chill, Izzy. Anyone would think you were the one getting married.'

'Cold day in hell,' Izzy murmured without heat. Good luck to Rachel and her Ben, but, though having a baby had changed her view on some things, her certainty that marriage was not for her remained unshakeable. She had read the statistics and in her view you'd have to be a gambler or a hopeless romantic to take those sorts of risks and she wasn't either.

It wasn't that she didn't believe in soul mates, but in her view if two people were meant to be together they shouldn't need a piece of paper to keep them that way.

'Don't worry, your Prince Charming is out there somewhere, Izzy—always supposing you don't take the treat-them-mean-keep-them-keen thing too far.'

'I don't!'

Unable to defend herself further because an expectant hush had fallen, Izzy slid into her own seat and waited as the other seated occupants passed her daughter along the row, like a smiling parcel. Lily landed in her lap happy and smiling.

Izzy glowed with pride as she received a gummy grin. Her daughter really was the most perfect baby.

Beside her, Rory's mother, Michelle Fitzgerald, looked amused as Lily made a bid for the blue feather fascinator it had taken Izzy half an hour to attach attractively in the chestnut brown hair she had pinned up in a simple twist. But even with a dozen hairpins the artistic loose tendrils had been joined by numerous wispy strands despite a double dose of hairspray. Her hair just had a mind of its own.

'Rory!' Michelle snapped, turning her attention to her son, who had still not taken his seat.

'All right, Ma,' he soothed with an eye roll as he dropped down into the pew next to Izzy.

'Rory, perhaps we should swap?' Izzy suggested as she abandoned her attempt to secure her headgear to the slippery surface of her shiny hair. Instead she shoved it in her pocket and offered a toy duck to Lily to distract her. 'In case Lily kicks off and I have to make a quick exit.'

She would have hated her small daughter to ruin the bride's big moment and, though she was for the most part a sunny baby, Lily was capable of some seismic meltdowns when thwarted.

According to Michelle it was just a phase all babies went through, and as much as Izzy respected the older woman's knowledge of all things baby she privately wondered if it was possible her daughter had inherited her volatile temperament from her father.

But that was one thing Izzy would never know, because although she knew every angle and shadow, every curve and plane of his face, as page after page in her sketchbooks filled with his likeness attested, Izzy didn't know the name of the man who had fathered her child.

She had not thought seriously about the day when Lily asked about her father—nothing beyond its inevitability. Maybe she would get her sketchbooks out on that day and show her daughter. Would she say, *'This is how he looked. He was possibly the most handsome man ever to draw breath...oh, and he smelt good too...'* Who knew? Since Lily's birth Izzy had adopted a one-day-at-a-time approach to life.

In the meantime she viewed the sketches as a cathartic coping mechanism. Her sketches were her therapy and one day presumably she would draw him out of her system.

'Sure, if you like.' Rory stood up, ducking his head in an attempt to appear inconspicuous, hard when you were a lanky six four. 'You two haven't met, have you?' he added, turning as he spoke to let Izzy shuffle along the wooden pew. 'Izzy, this is Roman Petrelli. He's here to buy some horses... Dad hopes. Do you remember Gianni arranged for that placement for me with Roman's Paris office last summer? Roman, this is my sister Izzy.'

Last summer she had been knee deep in nappies and night feeds and pretty much everything else had passed her by, but she did find it easy to place the handsome half-Italian Gianni among the plethora of Fitzgerald cousins. And there were a lot of cousins—her father was one of nine siblings.

'Hello.' A distracted smile curving her lips, she turned her head, following the direction of Rory's introductory nod, and her eyes connected, her smile wobbled and vanished.

She had walked right past him. How did that happen?

He was not the sort of man that under normal circumstances would be overlooked—Izzy hadn't the first time she had seen him.

Now he was here the breath left her lungs in a silent hiss of shock.

'Hello.'

The voice awoke dormant memories and sent a flash of heat through her body. Incapable of speech, she nodded and thought, *He really does have the longest eyelashes I have ever seen.* And there was no discernible recognition in the pitch-dark eyes those lashes framed.

This wasn't happening.

But it was! It was him—the man she had spent that night with.

Two years later and Izzy had rationalised the reckless impulse that had made her act so totally out of character. There was probably some psychological term for what she'd done when she'd been half out of her head with grief, exhaustion and shock, but Izzy had not continued to analyse it, she had simply drawn a line under it.

You could only beat yourself up so much and, as she had felt no desire since that night to rip off any man's clothes and ravish him, there had been no lasting consequences to her actions—except one, which she could never regret.

How could she regret something that had given her not just her much-loved daughter but a new and wonderfully supportive family? There was a strong possibility that, if she hadn't found herself alone, pregnant and very aware how fragile life was, the letter sent by the father she had never met might have stayed where she had initially thrown it—in the bin.

Tapping into reserves of self-control she didn't even know she possessed, the silly smile still pasted on her face, Izzy broke free of the pitch-black mesmerising stare and turned away. Outwardly calm, at least to the casual observer, her body was gripped by a succession of deep internal tremors as she hugged her daughter.

Her shoulder blades ached with tension as she buried her face in Lily's soft dusky curls. People often remarked on her vibrant colouring, marvelling at the peachy glow of her skin and her liquid dark eyes. The less tactful asked outright if she looked like her father.

Izzy never reacted to the question and her silence had given rise to a great deal of speculation. There were currently several theories in circulation about Lily's father, which ranged from him being a dead war hero to him being a married politician. But whatever people thought, the generally held opinion was that Izzy was the innocent party, the girl who had been abandoned, because apparently she came across as a nice girl.

The irony was not lost on her and Izzy detested the undeserved victim status that had been thrust on her, but, short of publicly announcing that she was actually a shameless trollop, what choice did she have?

It was actually a relief when someone chose to take her to task about her single-parent status. Just the previous evening Michael's great-aunt Maeve had exclaimed, 'A child needs two parents, young lady.'

'In a perfect world, yes, but the world isn't perfect and neither am I.'

Izzy's quietly dignified response had taken the wind out of the old lady's sails, but she had made a quick recovery. 'In my day a girl like you wouldn't be wandering around as bold as brass like she has nothing to be ashamed of.'

'She doesn't have anything to be ashamed of, Aunt Maeve.' It was her father who came to Izzy's rescue, putting an arm around her and drawing her in close.

'Don't you go looking at me like that, Michael. One of the few good things about being old is being as rude as I like—would you deprive me of one of my last pleasures?' She held out her empty glass and glanced at the whisky bottle on the dresser. 'So, girl, who is the father?'

Izzy had not satisfied the old lady's curiosity. She hadn't told anyone the identity of the father—how could she?

Izzy's blue eyes were shadowed with shamed anguish as she responded to Lily's cry of protest and loosened her grip just as the organist pulled out all the stops. Izzy knew better than most what it was like to grow up without a father and it was something she had always vowed not to do to a child of hers should she ever have one.

With the rest of the congregation Izzy rose to her feet. Were his eyes trained on the exposed nape of her neck or was it her guilty conscience that made her skin prickle and tingle? Tingle the way his long fingers had once made her—she pushed the thought away and took a deep breath. With Lily on one hip, she stared blankly at the service sheet clutched in her free hand, knowing she was a whisper away from tipping over into outright gibbering panic.

She had to stay calm.

She had to think.

The father of her baby was sitting behind her. What was she meant to do now?

Take a leaf out of her mother's book and write him a letter?

Casually drop into the conversation, *Oh, by the way, this is your daughter*? Now that would be a real ice breaker, but could it be listed under small talk?

She choked on a bubble of hysterical laughter, the sound drowned out by the hymn being sung.

Realistically Izzy knew, always had known, that should this unlikely event occur she had to accept the real possibility that he might not even remember that night two years ago. So maybe doing nothing was a possibility? Just wait and if he said nothing leave it…?

She reluctantly discarded the tempting idea. This was Lily's father. What had Rory called him…Roman? At least she had a name now and knew that he was Italian, although she'd already had an idea about his nationality. During their night together he had whispered wonderful things to her in throes of passion; she might not have understood the things he had said, but she had recognised the language.

She remembered everything.

She tried to push away the hot, erotic images crowding in—she had to focus.

On what, Izzy—your impending public humiliation?

Her chin lifted. She would take what was coming, but not Lily. She would protect Lily.

Lily, who looked so like her father, which was good news for her because she'd grow up to be the female version of him—stunning—but bad news because surely everyone seeing them together would know.

And he'd seen Lily.

He had to know!

Was he sitting there in shock?

No point speculating; she just had to stay calm and play this by ear. A wedding was hardly the place to introduce a man to his daughter.

Was there a good place?

He might be here with his girlfriend or wife

even…! Feeling sick now, Izzy closed her eyes and tried to remember who had been sitting next to him, but couldn't.

Could things get any worse? She'd slept with a stranger and got pregnant—please let him not have been married!

A question that might have been better asked before you ripped off his shirt.

Ignoring the sly insert of her conscience or what was left of it, Izzy touched a protective hand to her nape.

Nothing in his expression had suggested he even recognised her. Was it really possible he didn't remember their night together? Or maybe he might have developed a convenient amnesia to avoid embarrassment. If so should she play along with it? Everything in Izzy rebelled against the idea.

Why was she torturing herself? He might feel even worse and as embarrassed about that night as she was, sitting there now wondering if she was a potential bunny boiler about to mess up his life.

If so he'd feel relieved when he realised she didn't want anything from him. Rich men could be pretty protective of their wealth and she could recall now the word billionaire coming into the conversation when the family had discussed Rory's good fortune at securing a placement within the Petrelli company.

Great, she couldn't have had a one-night stand with a teacher or a plumber. No, she had to pick out a billionaire Italian!

At the end of the ceremony Izzy got to her feet when everyone else did, clutching her daughter to her chest. She slung a furtive look over her shoulders but chickened out at the last minute and tucked herself in between Rory and Emma in the slow-moving file of guests leaving the church, doing her best to be invisible. When she finally worked up the courage to look again Roman Petrelli was gone, the occupants of the pew behind having already vacated their seats.

She touched Rory's sleeve. Her half-brother turned his head. 'Your friend…is he?'

'Friend…? I do have more than one…?'

'Duh!' Emma, who was eavesdropping, inserted with a roll of her eyes. 'Who do you think she's talking about? The utterly gorgeous hunk, Roman, of course! Such a sexy name, but not as sexy as the man himself. Did you get a look at his eyes?' She pressed a hand to her heart and sighed dramatically. 'You know, I could really do with a walk on the wild side.'

'Izzy isn't as shallow as you,' her brother retorted, adding, 'Could you do with a hand there, Izzy?'

'Thanks.' Izzy slanted a grateful smile at her half-brother as she relinquished a squirming Lily to him. 'She wants to get down and she's really strong.'

'Me, shallow—I like that,' Emma interrupted, adding with a warm look at Lily, who was pulling her uncle's nose, 'All the Fitzgerald women are strong.' She sent a conspiratorial grin to Izzy. 'The only place Rory is Roman Petrelli's friend,' Emma confided, directing a sisterly smile of sweet malice at her brother, 'is in his dreams.

Rory only asked for him to be invited because he wants to suck up. Do you really think he's going to give a geek like you a job, Rory?'

'I'm a geek with a mind like a steel trap and great charm—why wouldn't the man give me a job?'

'As if!'

'Let's put it this way, little sister, I'm more likely to get a job off him than you are a night of passion.'

'Wanna bet?' Emma drawled, her eyes sparkling challenge.

'Like taking money off a baby.'

Izzy shook her head to clear the images flying around like a swarm of wasps in her brain. Images that involved her lovely innocent half-sister and a predatory Roman Petrelli. The sick feeling they left in the pit of her stomach had nothing to do with jealousy, she told herself in response to the nip of guilt. She was simply looking out for her sister.

Emma was only eighteen and was not nearly as sophisticated as she liked to pretend, and Roman

Petrelli was…an image of him lying on the bed, the toned musculature of his bronzed torso delineated by a sheen of sweat, flashed into her head and the word that came to her was…perfect.

'Please,' she reproached. Her laughter sounded forced to her own ears but the squabbling siblings didn't seem to notice. They just grinned and continued the argument until they got outside into the fresh air and the stakes in their bet had reached the extreme scale of silly.

'Let me have Lily,' Emma begged as they stepped aside to join the other guests in the sun.

'No, better not, Emma—she'll ruin your hair, and that dress…' Izzy pointed out, holding out her arms to take her daughter.

'Good point!' agreed Emma. 'I must look beautiful for Roman… How old do you think he is?'

'Too old for you,' retorted her brother austerely. 'And actually, Em, we're both out of luck. He's not coming to the reception so neither of us will be able to use our lethal charm.'

The reprieve might be temporary but the relief

was so intense Izzy laughed out loud, drawing a questioning look from her siblings.

'Don't look now—Aunt Maeve is heading this way.' Not a lie as such, more an inspired distraction, and it worked perfectly. At the mention of their elderly relative the sister and brother act adopted the attitude of sprinters under starter's orders.

'Just us again,' Izzy said, rubbing her nose against Lily's button nose and breathing in the sweet baby fragrance of her shampoo.

A wave of love so intense that she could hardly breathe closed Izzy's throat as she whispered softly, 'I'll never let anything hurt you. I love you, Lily baba.'

Izzy had known she had been loved, even though her mother had never said the words and not encouraged Izzy to be sentimental. A mother herself now, Izzy found it sad, but was relieved that her own fears that she might struggle to express her feelings had been unfounded. Since the first moment she had held her baby in her arms they were words she couldn't stop saying.

CHAPTER TWO

ROMAN'S intention when he'd walked into the church had been to skip the wedding reception—the deal for the new stallion had been done with Michael Fitzgerald and there was no longer a need to hang around. But his plans had now changed.

The adrenaline that had been dumped in his bloodstream when he'd recognised the slim woman walking up the aisle was still making him buzz, and, conscious of the fine tremor in his fingers, he pushed his hands deep into the pockets of his well-cut trousers.

She had been sitting right in front of him and all he'd had to do was reach out and he could have touched her. He knew who she was now, she had a name, and this time she wouldn't be able to vanish. Anticipation made him feel more alive than he had in…?

With a frown he blocked the thought. He'd been given a second chance on life and admitting he was bored seemed terminally ungrateful.

And in truth he wasn't bored. The mystery woman who was no longer a mystery represented a challenge—unfinished business.

Challenge, he decided, was the operative word. It wasn't as if she had occupied his thoughts to the exclusion of everything else since their night together, but her unexpected reappearance had resurrected the frustration her vanishing act had inflicted two years earlier. But he'd had more to worry about at the time than a one-night stand slipping away. Maybe his overreaction had been in part bruised ego or maybe she had become the focus for all his frustration at the time?

But then what man wouldn't feel frustrated when, having discovered the girl who ticked just about every erotic fantasy box he had, and some he didn't know he had, vanished off the face of the earth leaving nothing but the elusive fragrance of her warm skin on the bed sheets?

Roman had felt robbed and cheated. It had not even crossed his mind that he would not be able to persuade her to spend the rest of the day in bed with him. The idea that she wouldn't be there when he returned with coffee and croissants had not occurred to him.

Conscious of the heavy heat in his groin, he waited for her to appear again, his impatience growing until he began to wonder if he had imagined the whole thing.

It wouldn't be the first time.

There had been a couple of occasions when he had thought he had caught sight of her in the distance only to get closer and discover that the rich chestnut hair and slim petite curves belonged to someone else, someone who didn't have a mouth that invited sin.

This time, though, it was different; she was no figment of his imagination and she had recognised him. Admittedly her reaction had not quite been the one he normally got from women—

none, as far as he could recall, had ever looked as if they wanted to crawl under a pew.

She had blushed…actually blushed! His expressive lips quirked into a sardonic grin as he remembered her total lack of inhibition, her throaty little gasps and greedy clever hands. His mystery woman was the last person he would have imagined capable of blushing!

But the blush was in keeping with the entire freshly scrubbed, wholesome, sexy thing she had going on. Roman shrugged, closing off this line of speculation. He didn't care if she led a double life; he just wanted her, wanted to see her soft creamy body in his bed, feel her hands on him and feel her under him. He half resented wanting her, recognising that not having her could transform her from a missed opportunity to a mild obsession.

But something about her reaction still nagged at him. Why had bumping into an ex-lover thrown her into such a state of obvious confusion?

Unless she had a jealous partner around—even sitting next to her?

Who had been sitting next to her?

Roman, who was famed for his powers of observation, scrunched his brow in concentration as he tried to recall, but came up empty. He could remember the nape of her neck pretty well and the fall of the wisps of her hair around her face. The truth was he hadn't been thinking straight in the church and he'd needed the fresh air and distance to get his brain back in gear and his hormones on a leash.

Was she concerned he would not be discreet?

If so she needn't have worried. The only thing that Roman was interested in was having her in his bed again, not advertising the fact. Would the reality live up to his dreams or would he be disappointed? The anticipation of having his sexual curiosity satisfied on this point sent his level of arousal up another painful notch.

Roman continued his vigil of the guests from under the canopy of a leafy oak tree a safe distance away from his fellow guests clustered now in laughing groups around the newly married couple. His new vantage point gave him a clear view of the stragglers emerging from the church.

His tension and frustration grew with each passing moment, until Roman began to think somehow she had escaped him again. But then he saw her emerge.

Lust slammed through his body with the force of a sledgehammer. Watching her with the intensity of a hawk observing its prey, Roman felt his anger surge along with his appetite for her as he recalled the morning after their night together…

He had been so eager to get back into bed with her after his quick trip to the coffee shop that he had left his discarded clothes in a trail from the front door to the bedroom, only to find the bed empty and the sheets still warm—he had just missed her!

No woman had ever rejected him and now twice within the space of twenty-four hours a woman had walked out on him. Literally speaking he'd done the walking on the first occasion, and bizarrely it had been this second act of rejection that had got to him more. It had propelled him out into a city of millions of people to find her, which was either a measure of the sexual spell this woman had cast over him or a measure of his emotional stability at the time.

But he hadn't been insane when he'd walked into the crowded bar that night and the last thing he had been looking for was sex. His hand slid to his leg as he again thought back to the events of that night. He'd been licking his wounds and feeling pathetically sorry for himself.

Oh, God, yes, he had been pretty mad at the world, life and women as he'd sat at that table with a drink in front of him. He'd lost count of how many drinks had gone before it, when she had walked in.

He had sworn off women, but he'd noticed her, as had half the men in the room. He had drunk too much, but hadn't been drunk enough not to appreciate the shapely length of her slim toned thighs and the lush curves of her pert bottom in the dark pencil skirt she had worn. As he'd watched her move across the room he'd tugged the tie around his neck loose and thought, *One door closes and another opens.* Love had no longer been an integral part of his plan for the future, but he'd realised there was still sex.

It had been a cheering thought, one that might make a man get out of bed in the morning. For the months of his illness and subsequent chemo his libido had lain dormant, he hadn't even thought about sex, but things had woken up dramatically—he had wanted her from the moment he saw her.

She had great legs and a great body—slim and supple; that much he could tell even though she'd had more clothes on than ninety per cent of the women in the room. The skirt she had worn reached her knee and her elegant cream silk blouse had been more office wear than nightclub, yet she had exuded some innate sensuality—he hadn't been able to take his eyes off her.

Their night together had been incredible and the fact that he had experienced more pleasure making love to a woman he felt nothing for than any before or since had proved to him that emotional involvement did not enhance sex. His recent disastrous engagement only illustrated that it was actually an encumbrance.

Roman had never managed to recreate anything approaching the hot, sizzling sex he had enjoyed with his mystery woman. And he hadn't had sex for...not since... His brows lifted in surprise—he hadn't realised it had been that long!

He'd just been too busy with work lately to notice. The six months he had taken off on medical advice as he'd gone through his treatment had always seemed excessive and had necessitated him delegating areas of responsibility.

He had adopted a less hands-on approach that should have given him more time to enjoy his life—a healthier work-leisure balance. In reality he'd found himself unable to let go. Spare time was for people who didn't enjoy work or people with families and that was never going to be him.

On an intellectual level he knew that not being able to father a child did not make him any less a man, but it was not something a man felt on an intellectual level. When Roman had been given the news he had felt it in an icy fist in his gut, and even worse had been the prospect of telling his fiancée at that time, Lauren.

His lips twisted into a sardonic grimace as he played the scene over again in his head. Her understanding and support at the time had made him feel he might have misjudged her, but later he had discovered that not having children did not fill her with nearly the same sort of horror as the thought of how much weight she might put on during pregnancy.

Roman clenched his jaw and pushed away the thoughts—they belonged in another lifetime. His hungry gaze riveted on Izzy Fitzgerald again. She belonged in another lifetime too, but the memory of their night together had not faded, instead it had become something of a standard that he had measured every sexual encounter against since, and none had come near... Would the memory have exerted the same sort of fascination if he had known her name back then? He didn't have a clue, but he knew that he wanted her. He didn't waste time trying to figure out why. Time-wasting was anathema to Roman, who knew better than most what a precious commodity it was.

He could see the dark hair of the baby in her arms. Was it hers?

Roman did not do single mothers. Call him a cynic, but he could never quite believe that they were not out to bag a father for their child. Besides, he would be expected to pretend an interest in their kid and that just wasn't his thing. The fact was there were a lot of women who didn't come with the added complication of a child—so why complicate life?

But if Izzy Fitzgerald had a kid, would that be a deal breaker?

He smiled to himself as he watched her move, the wind plastering the blue dress she wore against the slender line of her legs. His temperature climbed several degrees as he remembered those legs wrapped around him, her nails digging into his shoulders, the expression of fierce concentration on her face as she fought her way towards climax.

He expelled a deep sigh. *Dio*, there were definitely exceptions to every rule. Did she have a husband? His brows twitched into a heavy frown; some rules he would not break.

But, God, it was going to kill him to walk away from this.

She had been the best sex he had ever had.

Izzy was about to get into one of the waiting cars that were lined up to whisk them to the reception when she realised that she didn't have her handbag; her keys and phone were in it.

'Damn, I think I left it in the church.'

Emma, who was standing with a shoe in one hand while she rubbed the toes of her shoeless foot with the other, looked up. 'Have you lost something, Izzy?'

'My bag—I think I left it in the church.'

Michelle, who was already in the car, leaned out with her arms outstretched. 'Give me Lily while you go and get it. You only have yourself to blame, Emma. I told you those heels were too high.'

'Thanks,' Izzy said, handing her daughter over

to the willing hands. 'Don't wait for me.' Izzy blew a kiss to her daughter and mouthed, 'I'll catch up,' through the closed window.

Michelle nodded, and her father, who was strapping Lily into a baby seat, waved. Izzy grinned in response before she began to retrace her steps back to the church. The hotel where the reception was being held was only a gentle stroll down the village high street and it wouldn't take her long to meet up with the rest of the family.

Izzy pushed open the lychgate and ran on into the churchyard, which was totally deserted but for a solitary figure, the vicar, who was making his way on foot to the reception. She exchanged a few words with him before she went back inside the church, the quiet of the building acting as a balm to her frayed nerves.

The prospect of contacting Lily's father and telling him she existed filled her with total dread, and then…then what? How would he react? How did she want him to react? Izzy clenched her hands into fists and wished fiercely that she had never learnt of his identity, that he had remained some dark dream, and felt immediately guilty for being so selfish. Of all people she should know that it was wrong to deprive a child of all knowledge of her father.

She breathed a slow deep breath. She'd do the right thing—whatever that was—but not today. Today she would party, dance and enjoy herself.

Izzy laughed, the sound echoing back at her as she thought, *Who am I fooling?* She could almost feel the draft from the proverbial sword hanging by a thread above her head.

Her handbag was not on the pew where she thought she had left it, but a quick frantic search revealed it on the floor where it had fallen and, other than a dusty footprint, it was none the worse for wear.

She dusted it off and once outside opened it to check the contents. She was just refastening the pretty pearl-encrusted clasp when a prickling on the back of her neck made her pause, and slowly she turned, lifting a hand to shade her eyes from the sun.

Somehow she wasn't surprised at all to see Roman Petrelli standing only a few feet away.

Her heart was thudding like a sledgehammer against her ribs as she straightened her slender shoulders and lifted her chin. That fictional sword suddenly felt very real indeed!

Her earlier glimpse of him had left her with the impression of extreme elegance and raw male power, and now she could see that he possessed both those qualities in abundance. She could also see just how breathtakingly handsome his classically cut clean-shaven features were.

Of course, she already knew he was good-looking. That night in the bar he had been elegant, but crumpled in a dark, brooding way, his jaw shadowed and his hair worn a lot shorter then, sticking up in spiky tufts.

Izzy had no idea what demons he had been struggling to contain, but she had seen it in his taut body language and the vulnerability she had sensed was there behind the hard reckless glow in his eyes.

She recognised it was possible that she had been

imagining something that had never been there, because she had needed an excuse for jumping into bed with him. But Izzy liked to think that she had been drawn to him, had felt that weird connection to him, because she had been fighting her own demons too.

There was no trace of vulnerability, hidden or otherwise, in the man who stood before her now. Here was a man definitely in control, a man who did not inspire any stirrings of empathy.

His eyes were sensuous, but cynical and hard. There was a hint of cruelty in the sculpted curve of his lips and she felt a shudder run down her spine. The only emotion this impeccably dressed, effortlessly elegant stranger inspired in Izzy was a deep unease that bordered antipathy. Her skin prickled with it.

'It was a lovely wedding,' she heard herself say inanely.

Roman studied her, searching for signs of the forthright, bold woman who had delighted him in bed with her directness. Many women had thrown themselves at him, but she had been different, or so it had seemed to him. She had seduced him, not just with her delicious body, but with her generosity and a rare utter lack of self-consciousness.

His jaw tightened and he realised that she could not even meet his eyes. He felt a stab of disappointment.

'We have been introduced—you probably don't remember. I'm Izzy.' She thought of holding out her hand but changed her mind and rubbed it up and down her thigh, the friction creating a static charge that made the fabric cling. Forget touching him, just being this close to him was painfully uncomfortable and her skin tingled with awareness, the muscles in her stomach quivering like an overstrung violin. Touching…no, not a good idea!

His sensually moulded lips thinned. How long would she continue with this little charade that they were strangers?

'I remember.'

The throaty comment was open to interpretation, but Izzy, struggling to stay in control, chose to treat it at face value. 'I believe Rory worked for you. He really enjoyed it.' Her jittery glance encompassed the empty churchyard; anything that meant she could legitimately not look at him was good. 'Everyone's made their way to the hotel.' Good manners made her add, 'Do you know the way? Can I help you?'

'I really hope so, Izzy, or is that Isabel?'

Her eyes flew to his face. She moistened her lips nervously with her tongue, struggling against the sensation that she was sinking beneath a wave of sexual awareness that was wrapping itself around her like an invisible straightjacket.

Breaking contact with his sardonic glittering stare, she conjured up a smile of sorts. 'Nobody calls me that.' She made a show of looking around. 'It's Izzy. Looks like we're the last…or are you not going to the reception?' she asked hopefully.

'Wild horses would not keep me away.'

'Really…oh, well, it's not far. Do you need a car?'

Without meaning to she dropped her glance to

his leg. She remembered the red livid scars she had seen gouged into the muscles of his thigh during their night together. She had been conscious of a slight limp when he had approached her in the bar, but had dismissed it until she had seen the cause. The scarred tissue had shocked her, causing her sensitive stomach to quiver in reaction to the obvious pain they represented.

'Thank you, but I think I can make it under my own steam,' he said. Instantly he was catapulted into the past as he remembered her gasp when she had first seen the scars that night two years ago.

Survivor's scars, he called them. They were not pretty now, but two years ago they had been relatively fresh; the livid purple puckered tracks gouged in his flesh had been the thing of horror movies. In his head he had anticipated her revulsion to them and had schooled himself not to care. It had only been his desire to see her that had stopped him turning off the light.

He had offered but she'd refused. She had lain on the bed where he had left her as he had removed his clothes. She had been laughing throatily after the shoe he had flung over his shoulder had hit a mirror, cracking it in a zigzag from top to bottom.

But when she had seen his scars she had stopped laughing and he had tensed. Pity as a reaction was even less attractive to him than repugnance.

Holding his eyes, she had flipped sinuously over onto her stomach and grabbed his wrist. Shaking her head, she had pulled his hand away from the lamp.

She had looked at the ugly red line that began high on his thigh and ended a few inches above his knee and asked, 'Does it hurt?' adding huskily when he shook his head, 'Can I touch…?'

'Touch?'

Roman had taken an involuntary step back. He had always taken his body, the perfect symmetry of his strong limbs and his naturally athletic physique, for granted, but all that had changed overnight. His body had betrayed him and become the enemy and though not a vain man he accepted that others would be repelled by his scars. For him they were a constant reminder not to take anything for granted—ever.

'Why would you want to? Morbid curiosity?'

Her astonishment had been too spontaneous to be feigned. 'Don't be stupid.'

'I am normally considered to be above average in the brains department.'

Her slow wicked smile had made the lust in his belly grip hard. 'I'm not that interested in your brains.'

Her blouse, unbuttoned to the waist, had billowed out as she'd pulled herself up onto her knees. He had been unable to take his eyes off her, the tantalising shadows of her nipples through the lace of the bra that matched her pants, as with sinuous grace she had risen from the bed and come to stand beside him. Barefooted she had come up to his shoulder. 'Are you hiding any more of those?'

He had been unprepared and shocked when she had reached out again and touched him, lightly running a finger down the raised scar tissue.

He had caught her wrist, unable to keep the bitterness from creeping into his voice as he'd asked, 'Isn't that enough?'

'No.' Tilting her head to look at him, she'd pulled her hand from his grip. 'Not nearly enough. I want to touch all of you,' she'd whispered. 'I don't want to miss any place out.'

Roman felt lust clutch hard and low in his belly and was dragged back to the here and now. A faint growl worked its way upwards from his chest before he managed to push the images away.

'We could always walk together.' Of all the things they could do together, walking was not high on his list, but he was not about to let her escape.

'Actually I'm in a bit of a hurry.'

He felt his exasperation climb. Dismay was not a response Roman was accustomed to from attractive young women, and he suspected the novelty value would wear off quickly.

'And you think I can't keep up?' He might not be taking the lead on any climbs, but his limp only manifested itself now when he was extremely fatigued.

'No, of course...' She took a deep breath and sighed. 'Fine.' Said with all the enthusiasm of someone who had just agreed to give up her place on the last lifeboat.

Roman was torn between amusement and annoyance at the grudging concession. His annoyance would have been a lot greater had he not known that she was as aware of the chemistry spark between them as he was, but for some reason she was reluctant to acknowledge it...

He was confident that whatever the reason for fighting the attraction she would lose the battle, and he relished the prospect of seeing the confident bold woman he knew was there under her diffident, fresh-faced exterior.

'A pleasant stroll down a leafy village road on a sunny day—what could be nicer?' murmured Roman as he fell in beside her, matching his stride to hers.

'The inn is fourteenth-century.'

'Is the tour commentary optional?'

She slid him a sideways look of dislike. He had no manners at all but a great profile. Her glance drifted lower. Actually he had a great everything. 'I thought you might be interested. My mistake.'

'I'm fine with the charming company and the leisurely stroll,' he murmured, adding drily, 'Very leisurely stroll.'

Izzy compressed her lips, and, to squash any suspicion he might have that she wanted to prolong this walk, lengthened her stride. It was a struggle, despite his comments to the contrary, to believe that his mangled leg did not give him pain, but he showed no sign of difficulty in matching her pace.

As they continued down the steep, winding village street a silence developed…not of the comfortable variety. In the end and despite the risk of drawing another of his rude comments, Izzy cleared her throat. She had to do something to drown out the silent tension.

'It was a lovely service… Rachel looked beautiful, didn't she?'

Roman, who thought one bride in a meringue

dress looked much like any other, gave a non-committal grunt. The main event had not been what he was watching, or thinking about. 'Her father is Michael's brother?'

Izzy, happy to discuss this safe subject, nodded. 'Yes, they moved to Cumbria about twenty years ago. They bought neighbouring farms and married sisters.' Both brothers still retained the Irish accent that Izzy found so attractive.

'So the bride is your cousin?'

'No...well, sort of, I suppose. Michelle isn't my mother—I'm not a real Fitzgerald.' Not something she normally said, actually not something she ever said except to herself, but he made her nervous and she babbled when she was nervous. He made her a lot of other things but Izzy didn't want to go there.

Roman registered that this was an odd thing to say, but as his interest in the Fitzgerald family and how she fitted into it was at best minimal he did not react to the information. Instead he suddenly stopped in his tracks. While it had been entertaining to a point he was tired of this fencing.

'How long are you going to carry on pretending we are strangers?'

Izzy took another few steps before she slowed and turned to face him, her face flaming. His elevated brow and his dark eyes mocked her.

'I didn't even know your name until five minutes ago. We are strangers.'

'Strangers who have had sex,' Roman retorted, his impatience wearing paper thin. Her innocent wide-eyed routine was beginning to irritate him. 'Was the child yours?' He had a vague recollection of dark curls and a pink dress, so presumably a girl, but he had been concentrating on the woman holding her and the way her already beautiful face had been transformed when she had smiled at the kid.

He'd said *yours* not *mine*. So maybe he hadn't guessed that Lily was his daughter. Feeling her panic subside from red alert to amber and fighting the lingering urge to run, Izzy veiled her eyes with her silky lashes as she fought to regain her composure.

'Yes, she is.'

'Are you married?'

Izzy was too startled to respond to his abrupt question. 'I beg your pardon.'

'I'd prefer you answered my question.'

There didn't seem much point lying. 'No, I'm not married,' she admitted.

He tipped his head, some of the tension in his expression fading as his eyes continued to sweep her face. 'And you're not with anyone?'

Izzy framed a cold smile in response to his continued abrupt questioning style. She was suddenly conscious of being very hot. The silk chiffon dress clung uncomfortably to her skin and beneath it her bra chafed her nipples.

'Is this you making small talk or is there a reason for this interrogation?' It was hard to tell if he knew how rude he was being.

'You didn't answer my question.'

She gave a small smile. 'You noticed.'

He clenched his teeth in a white smile that left

his spectacular eyes cold. 'I can do small talk. I can even tell you you're the most beautiful woman here today.'

Izzy was desensitised to insults after being the focus of gossip for so long, but compliments always threw her off balance, even one delivered in such an oddly dispassionate way. Or maybe it was the person doing the delivering.

She moved her head sharply to one side, causing the loose tendrils of her hair to move over her face, partly to hide the juvenile blush she felt burning. She looked at him through her lashes and achieved a negligent shrug that managed to deliver a level of indifference she was a million miles from feeling.

'You could? But your innate honesty prevents it?' she suggested.

'I could, but—' He shook his head and his hooded gaze skimmed the pure lines of her oval face, lingering on her soft full mouth, taking pleasure from her beauty on a purely aesthetic level. His pleasure tipped over into the carnal as the image of those cool lips moving over his body sent his level of arousal up several painful notches.

'After that build-up this should be good.' Her amused smile faded as their glances locked. The rampant, hungry gleam in his eyes made her painfully conscious of the ache between her thighs.

'It will be,' he promised modestly, adding in a low throaty drawl that made her heart kick heavily against her ribcage, 'I thought you'd prefer a more direct approach.'

She had been very direct the last time they'd met, and it had saved a lot of time. He really wanted that bold seductive witch back. What would it take to cut through this act? 'Maybe,' he mused, appearing to consider the question, 'I haven't been direct enough.'

Before she could digest his comment, let alone respond to it, he was right there beside her before she was even conscious of him moving. Then without a word he framed her face with one hand, fitting his thumb to the angle of her jaw, and tipped her face up to him. His other hand moved over the curve of her bottom, his fingers splayed across the firm contours as he dragged her closer to him, then in one smooth, seamless motion he fitted his mouth to hers.

Izzy froze at the contact, her body stiffening in tingling shock. Then as his tongue insinuated itself between her lips, forcing them apart, a low tremulous moan was wrenched from deep inside her. He was hard and hot and she closed her eyes, stopped fighting and grabbed for him, her hands circling his neck as she opened her mouth, inviting him to deepen the slow, sensual exploration.

The devastating kiss seemed to go on for ever, or was it seconds? Izzy had no idea. When he released her her head was spinning and she was shaking and struggling for breath. Blinking, she took a shaky step back, falling inelegantly off one heel in her agitation.

'No!' she cried, avoiding the steadying hand he had extended as she regained her balance—her pride and dignity would take a lot longer. What was it about this man that seemed to awake her inner cheap tart?

Shock and shame rippled through her as she stood there wanting to hit his smugly complacent face, wanting to curl up and die from sheer shame, wanting not to be here.

Shame or not, Izzy knew with despairing certainty that if he touched her she'd react the same way. She wrapped her arms tightly around herself as she shivered and blinked to clear the last remaining shreds of the hot haze of lust fogging her vision.

When she made herself look at him she felt something inside her snap. Not the same something that had snapped when he had slid his tongue into her mouth, not mind-numbing lust—this was mind-awakening fury. Two years...two years of coming to terms with that night and in a few seconds she was right back to square one!

'Just what was that meant to prove?' she yelled at him as her conscience criticised her. *You are such a hypocrite, Izzy. You are angry with him when you should be angry with yourself.* As she was hit by a fresh wave of shame her eyes fell.

He might have instigated the kiss but you sure as hell did your best to make sure it didn't end!

'That we are wasting our time talking when we should be in bed,' he answered calmly.

A gurgling sound of sheer disbelief escaped her clamped lips as the haze of lust descended again like a blanket. Furious with herself for inviting his response, she painted an expression of distaste onto her face while struggling to push away the images his words had planted in her head…sweat-glistening golden skin, tangles of limbs pale and dark intertwined…moans… She wasn't even sure if the moan was part of her torrid imaginings or real. All she cared about at this point was keeping him ignorant of what was going on in her head.

'My God, you do love yourself, don't you?' Her haughty scorn was paper thin; scratch the surface and her entire body was suffused with burning heat. Her insides shuddered with the aftershocks that still made her shake.

At least no one had seen them; that was something. The thought was barely formed before a frantically barking dog ran out into the street. Izzy immediately recognised it as the shop owner's excitable terrier.

Afraid that the noise might bring someone out of the shop to investigate, she snapped a desperate, 'Hush, Bella,' which the dog ignored as she ran barking towards the village shop where she continued to bark as she danced around the feet of the figure standing in the doorway.

Izzy's heart sank to her knees as she registered the familiar figure of Emma, her eyes round with shock and her mouth open.

'Izzy!' she said as though she expected to be contradicted, her glance moving repeatedly back and forth between Izzy and the tall figure beside her.

'This isn't what it looks like, Emma.' Except it was, it was exactly what it looked like, and this time she didn't have trauma or alcohol to blame. It had been all her. Biting her lip, she turned to Roman, her blue gaze willing him to back her up. 'Tell her,' she snapped.

'I don't know what it looked like. I only know

what it felt like—rather good. You haven't lost your touch, *cara*.'

In one sentence he had managed not only to confirm Emma's suspicions, but also leave the impression that this wasn't the first time they'd kissed.

Her eyes narrowed with dislike, and to rub salt in the wound he looked utterly cool, except for the dark bands of colour that drew attention to the slashing angle of his sculpted cheekbones.

Emma shook her head as though she were just waking up. 'Wow, you and…' She inhaled and suddenly grinned, approval beaming all over her face. 'I said you needed some fun but I never…' She looked at Roman and shook her head again, framing a silent Wow! behind her hand as she looked at her sister.

'Emma, no, I—'

'It's fine, Izzy, totally cool. The man obviously prefers brunettes. Carry on, pretend I was never here.' Throwing a quick cheeky grin over her shoulder, she set off down the hill as fast as her incredibly high spiky heels would take her.

'Emma!' Acting on an instinct that told her she had to stop Emma and explain to her that she couldn't tell anyone what she had seen, Izzy hit the ground running, but she had barely covered a yard before she was physically hauled back.

Slapping at the restraining hand on her shoulder, she spun around furiously. 'What do you think you are doing?' she snapped.

He released his grip on her arm but took both her hands in his, pulling her around to face him. 'What are you doing?' he countered, struggling to drag his eyes above the level of her heaving bosom.

'I've got to stop her before she tells someone that she saw us.'

Under his olive-toned skin the fine muscles along his jaw quivered and clenched. 'You have a baby so I'm thinking people might have guessed you've been kissed before,' he drawled.

'I'm sure you thrive on notoriety, but I'll still be living here tomorrow.'

'Why do you assume I thrive on notoriety?' Roman worked very hard to protect his privacy.

She shook her head stubbornly. 'You're a billionaire p-playboy.'

The term made Roman's firm lips twitch with amusement. 'Playboy?'

'All right, maybe not a playboy,' she admitted. Did she even know what a playboy was? 'But you are a billionaire.'

Roman blinked. He had been referred to as such before but never so accusingly. 'Which means I don't value my privacy...?' The furrow between his dark brows deepened as he tacked on an abrupt questioning, 'And why?'

She looked at him blankly. 'What do you mean why? Why what?'

'Why will you be here tomorrow? Didn't you live in London? Why have you buried yourself out here in the middle of nowhere?' Unless she had followed the father of her child?

'You can't bring up a child in a flat...' *Why am I defending my life decisions to him?* 'And anyway, this happens to be a very good place to live.'

'So this is a permanent arrangement?'

Her eyes slid from his. 'My family lives here.'

She lifted her hands, still confined in his. 'Do you mind? I need to catch up with Emma.'

He let her go and watched as she rubbed her wrists even though he had not been holding her tightly. 'You catch her and what? What are you going to do to her if she doesn't keep your dirty little secret?'

For the first time she picked up on the anger in his voice.

'What's going to happen if she does tell? Is the sky going to fall in?'

Izzy loosed a scornful laugh. 'Oh, I'm sorry, I wouldn't want to hurt your ego by not telling the world what a great kisser you are. Would it help if I gave you marks out of ten?' She rolled her eyes. 'Oh, for goodness' sake,' she snapped. 'Get out of my way. I have better things to do than pander to your massive ego. I have a baby who needs feeding.'

The reminder of the child situation brought a frown to his broad brow. If he could not have a child of his own Roman did not want to play father to some other man's…but he was willing to concede that all rules had exceptions.

'Look, two years ago I was a very different person. Let me spell it out for you: I don't have sex with rude, incredibly arrogant bores.'

'You did.'

She gritted her teeth. 'I must have been very drunk.'

'No, you weren't, but you were incredible.'

Furious with herself for reacting to his smoky voice, she screened her eyes and took a deep breath, exhaling it slowly before she reacted.

'Really.' She gave a rueful grimace. 'I'll have to take your word for it. I'm afraid that it's all a bit hazy for me.'

'I am happy to refresh your memory. I've wanted to repeat the experience for a long time.'

The man had an extraordinary ability to say the most outrageous things the way other people commented on the weather.

'You want to get drunk and jump into bed with a total stranger? I don't suppose there's anything stopping you, but personally I like to learn from bad experiences, not repeat them.'

'Bad experience? How would you know if you don't remember?'

'I've met you now, so let's call it a lucky guess.' Izzy's hands balled into fists at her sides as she struggled to breathe past the anger building in her chest. Did he really think she was that easy?

No, he knows *you're that easy.*

'Anyway, what are you suggesting—the shrubbery?' She flicked the bush to her right with her hand, causing scarlet petals from the rhododendrons to rain on the floor. 'Or is that too romantic? What about the back seat of your car?'

One expressive brow lifted. 'I have a perfectly acceptable hotel room, but I'm always up for a new experience.'

Izzy looked at him, achieving a look of amused contempt, then spoilt it by choking out, 'You're totally disgusting!'

He looked taken aback by her reaction. 'I thought you liked me that way.'

Like! Like had nothing whatever to do with the

feelings this man evoked in her. 'I didn't say that or anything like it!'

Again her lie returned to taunt her. 'How would you know, if you don't remember anything about it? I'm not quite sure why you're getting so worked up. I thought you were a girl who liked to cut to the chase.'

'I know you think you're totally irresistible, but for the record I find you crude and crass and quite frankly I wouldn't touch you with a ten-foot pole!'

'Actually, I'm thinking more hands-on, *cara*,' he drawled. 'So you're not interested?'

His amused disbelief made her long to slap his complacent, beautiful face. 'Absolutely definitely not.'

He shrugged. 'A pity.'

Izzy couldn't decide if she was relieved or insulted that he wasn't pushing the idea. The fact that she had doubt at all proved that her judgement was seriously flawed around this man.

CHAPTER THREE

Izzy walked into the hotel foyer, aware that Roman was following a few steps behind her. She stopped and turned. 'Will you go away? Or I'll call Security.'

'I was invited, remember!'

'You…'

'All right, I'm going, but if you change your mind I have a room…'

She ground her teeth at his deliberate provocation. 'I'm never going to be that drunk.'

'Izzy, dear, did you find it?'

Flustered, Izzy turned to find Michelle with Lily in her arms, walking across the lobby towards her. 'Find…? Oh, yes, my bag, thanks, Michelle. None the worse for—' She stopped and dropped her hand, realising that she had found her bag, but she didn't have a clue where it was now. Although she wasn't much concerned compared with the presence of Roman Petrelli, who was now standing just a few feet away from his daughter. 'Sorry, it took me longer than I thought.' She knew he hadn't moved; even with her back to him she could feel the waves of raw male magnetism he radiated.

'Oh, don't worry about that, the reception isn't for another hour.' Michelle's expression showed her opinion of this break with tradition. 'All at the behest of that ridiculously expensive photographer Rachel insisted on.'

'Well, thanks. I didn't mean to dump her on you.'

'You know I love having her, the little angel. Actually she fell asleep in the car and she's only just woken up. Have you got her…yes?' Michelle relinquished her hold on the baby and took a step back to grab a glass of champagne from the tray of a passing waiter.

'Have you seen Emma?' Izzy asked casually.

'No, she must be around somewhere. Are you feeling all right, Izzy? You look rather pale. You haven't got another migraine—' She broke off, her quizzical gaze shifting to a point behind Izzy. Even without the eyes-widening moment that Izzy presumed was the normal response for any female with a pulse when they saw Roman, she knew what was coming next, but even so she still flinched when she heard his voice.

'Excuse me, ladies.' Moving into view he divided his smile between Izzy and Michelle, giving the older woman the lion's share and conscious in his peripheral vision of Izzy's expression of panic. What the hell was her problem? Did she really think he was about to tell the world they had shared a night of passion? Being associated with him had never done any woman's social standing any harm. 'But I think this might be yours…?'

If her back hadn't been literally to the wall Izzy had no doubt she would have run, but as the tall, elegant and devastatingly handsome figure approached, with a smile that could have charmed a steel bar into malleable submission, there was nowhere for her to go.

Izzy took a deep breath and lifted her chin. This was face-the-music time. She stared at the handbag dangling by its decorative metal chain strap from the long brown forefinger of his right hand, but before she could respond Michelle exclaimed, 'Oh, look, Izzy—it's your bag!'

Izzy, who had never seen Roman turn on the charm before, was not surprised to hear the older woman give a girlish giggle.

'Oh, yes, so it is. I must have dropped it again or something, thank you.' She waited, her eyes conveying cold disdain as she shifted Lily's weight to her left hip and in the process partially shielded her from view before she extended a hand to receive it.

Roman held the bag just a little away, prolonging the moment before he threaded it over her wrist. His lips twitched appreciatively; managing to make 'thank you' sound like 'go to hell' was quite an achievement.

He dipped his dark glossy head. 'You're welcome.'

'Well, isn't that lucky you found it, and realised

it was Izzy's?' From Michelle's expression it was clear that she was not immune to his high-voltage charm.

'Very lucky.' He extended his hand towards Michelle. 'Roman Petrelli. We have met at Gianni's wedding.'

For once Izzy was able to place Emma and Rory's handsome older cousin as the son of her father's eldest brother. He was here today with his gorgeous, red-headed, very pregnant wife.

'Of course, you were his best man, but no.' Michelle tilted her head a little to one side as she studied Roman's handsome features with a frown. 'That's not it. You remind me of some-one…?'

Izzy knew exactly who he reminded her of and stared at the floor. This was probably what it felt like to act normally in the middle of an earth-quake when you knew, you just *knew*, that any moment the earth was going to open at your feet.

'Your son Rory worked for me last summer… we were impressed. He's a young man with promise.'

The perfect way to a mother's heart—say something good about her son, Izzy thought, a cynical smile twisting her lips.

'Thank you. I'm prejudiced, of course, but I know he really enjoyed working for your firm. He was so enthusiastic when he got home. He's waiting for his results at the moment. It's such a tough job market out there.'

'Has he put in many applications?' Roman asked, not thinking about applications but the slim figure standing a few feet away. He could feel the inexplicable anxiety rolling off her in waves.

'He's waiting for the results of his finals.' Michelle gave a rueful smile and admitted, 'He was aiming for a first, but he thinks he messed up a paper.'

'Well, exams are useful but I think enthusiasm and ambition are equally important.' Struggling to maintain a level of appropriate interest, Roman fished a card out of his pocket. 'My PA will be expecting his call.'

Izzy was amazed that Michelle, normally a

very moral person, saw nothing wrong in this piece of blatant bribery thinly disguised as generosity.

The man clearly thought he could buy his way in or out of any situation. He probably heard no as a response once every ten years or so and then it was probably incorporated into, No, I don't mind if you wipe your shiny handmade Italian shoes on me, Mr Petrelli. It would be an honour.

Izzy endured this conversation with gritted teeth. Without asking someone to move out of her way she could not drift unobtrusively away without drawing unwanted attention to herself and, more importantly, Lily.

She was cornered and couldn't even access the glasses of champagne, she mused as another waiter drifted by, and she could really do with a drink. She had always known Lily looked like her father but until seeing them virtually side by side she had not realised how much. She couldn't see how anyone would not be struck by the uncanny likeness.

He had to notice… It was inevitable. She was

amazed they weren't already the focus of finger pointing.

This was the last place in the world she wanted the big reveal, right here with a captive audience. It was going to happen; it was just a matter of when.

It was Lily herself who eventually kick-started the event. Tired of being carried and ignored, she let out a yell, shouting loudly, 'Want go down, play…now!'

Roman winced in response to the sudden high-pitched ear-piercing squeal.

Michelle saw his expression and said, 'She does have a temper!' as she gazed with a fondness he struggled to understand at the red-faced bundle who was struggling like a demented demon to escape her mother's arms.

His glance moved on to the small demon's mother, who looked self-conscious, pink-cheeked and actually far too young to be a mother as she struggled to soothe the child, whose tantrum was causing a good deal of attention.

Roman might have expected to feel a certain

amount of satisfaction witnessing her discomfiture. He did not consider himself a vindictive man, but he was a man who believed strongly in the old adage of 'what goes around comes around', and she had left him feeling a different and extremely painful type of discomfort. Her hypocrisy was staggering. First she had responded to him in a way that had fanned his smouldering desire into a full-scale conflagration, but had then acted as if he had somehow insulted her by suggesting they get reacquainted in bed! She had somehow managed to offend his masculinity and his intelligence in the process!

Double whammy!

Roman knew the signs when a woman was interested in him, and she was, so why was she acting as though there was some sort of stigma attached? It was as if she had undergone some weird personality transplant. Maybe taking her out of this environment, where relatives lurked around every corner, would bring back the erotic, uninhibited, adventurous lover of that night? He had a private jet on standby…and the villa on

Lake Como… He smiled, seeing the plan formulating in his head coming together.

The opportune timing of the child's sob meant he did not have time to consider why he felt such a strong need to construct an elaborate plan to get this woman into his bed, when he could achieve the same result without any effort on his part at all and with a woman who did not act as though he were a social liability!

As he watched Izzy cope with the distressed child and display a level of patience that was staggering, Roman found himself experiencing a sudden and inexplicable desire to help her.

He didn't, of course. He didn't have a clue about children, especially loud, screaming ones. His critical glance slid back to the child, who appeared to have been pacified slightly and was not so red in the face any more. He could see that she was not so… He stopped and looked closer. The child had dark hair, with blue-black curls, huge chocolate-brown eyes and skin the colour of rich honey. His eyes followed the suddenly very familiar shape of a jaw and eye…the mouth.

'*Dio!*'

Izzy was alerted to the impending scene by his raw gasp. Her glance flew to his face in time to witness the stunned recognition. Both shock and denial were written in the strong sculpted lines of his patrician face.

'How is this possible?'

Unaware that he had voiced the question out loud, Roman half expected to hear an answer in his head, but no reply was forthcoming. His brain, unable to cope with the shock, had closed down.

'Were you off school the day they did the birds and bees?' She regretted the comment the moment she said it, but flippancy was one of her coping mechanisms.

Jolted back to reality by Izzy's comment, Roman glared at her. What was she now...the mother of his child? It didn't seem possible, but instantly he knew it was. He looked at her and then at the baby, then back at the mother, who looked away guiltily.

'Isabel?'

His voice made the fine downy hairs on her body tingle… 'Izzy,' she corrected, staring at his chest. Almost without thought she saw herself unbuttoning his shirt and peeling back the fabric to expose the smooth, golden tautly muscled flesh beneath. Taking a deep breath, she closed the door on the memory.

His dark, heavy-lidded stare zeroed back in on her face. 'I think we need to talk.'

She gave a grudging nod, but was saved the need to respond by the appearance of a suited usher who had been sent to corral the stragglers and drive them into the wedding breakfast.

He consulted a seating plan in his hand and said, 'Come on, ladies, we need to get you in first. It's a tight squeeze and once you're at your table it's kind of hard to get out without a lot of hassle.'

The last sight Izzy had of Roman Petrelli's dark head was in the distance as she joined the file of guests who were waiting to be greeted by the happy couple.

He looked like the living, breathing incarnation of retribution.

* * *

The wedding breakfast seemed to go on for ever, but when the opportunity arose during a gap in the speeches Izzy made her move for the fire door and escaped into the hallway.

There was no one in sight.

Then she spotted his tall distinctive dark head at the same time a waiter extended a tray of champagne her way.

With a groan of, 'Oh, God, no!' that made the waiter withdraw his tray, she began to weave her way through the crowd, her aim nothing more complicated than to put as much space between herself and the tall Italian as was humanly possible. She walked through the first door she came to and found herself in an orangery that was for the moment blissfully empty except for an elderly man with a red nose and large moustache who was dozing in one sunny corner, and the pianist playing the baby grand in one corner of the room.

The pianist smiled at Izzy and glanced towards the sleeping figure before miming an ironic hushing motion with his finger.

Izzy smiled back and set her struggling daughter on the floor, rotating her neck muscles, which ached from a combination of extreme tension plus the extra pounds her growing daughter had gained.

'Careful,' she cautioned absently as Lily grabbed a chair leg and pulled herself to her feet.

Izzy leaned back in the wrought-iron chair and sighed as her daughter eyed a plant several feet away and launched herself towards it, managing half a dozen steps before falling on her well-padded bottom. The startled expression on her face drew a laugh from Izzy.

'Oops!'

Her daughter's lower lip stopped quivering and the tragedy vanished and a moment later she sent her mother a sunny grin and continued across the room on all fours this time. As she watched her progress Izzy's smile faded; she knew she was hiding and that she couldn't continue in this way.

What was she avoiding? She couldn't run away; she had to face him—he was Lily's father. The image of his expression when he had looked at

Lily surfaced, the shock and disbelief etched in his strong-boned features still fresh in her mind. She doubted many things in this supremely confident man's life had shaken him, but seeing Lily had.

Izzy suddenly felt an unexpected stab of sympathy for Roman. She had been shocked too, but she had had nine months to get used to the idea of having a child. He'd just had the facts thrust live and kicking under his nose.

God only knew what was going through his mind.

She took a deep calming breath. It felt like the first time she'd really thought clearly since she'd felt herself sinking into those deep dark eyes on that night two years ago.

That one night when she had been someone else, but a night she was reminded of every time she looked at her daughter. Sure, this had been a shock—massive understatement—but might it not also be a positive thing…a good thing? It was a massive disruption of the comfortable status quo she had been enjoying, but surely her daughter having a chance of something she had never had the opportunity to experience was worth some disruption?

'Lily, no!' Izzy raised her voice in warning above the soft piano music in the background.

Her daughter's head turned at the sound of her raised voice, but she did not halt her shuffling progress towards the tall cactus sporting scarlet blooms along its spiky stem that had caught her eye.

Before Izzy or her daughter could reach the spiky cactus the pot was blocked by a tall figure. A frustrated Lily treated the tall figure to a glare and, thrusting out her lower lip, yelled, 'No!'

Izzy took a deep calming breath and scooped up her daughter, sweeping her wriggling and kicking off the floor. 'Her favourite word.'

'She's determined, isn't she?' Roman observed, staring at the red-faced baby who was his daughter—how was it possible? He pushed away the question that had been running on a continual loop since the baby had looked at him.

He had always acknowledged a comment that

a baby looked like one parent or the other with a certain degree of polite scepticism. In his, admittedly limited, experience all babies looked much the same with their indistinct unformed features.

He had never had reason to change his mind about this until half an hour ago, but he could have been wrong—he had to be wrong.

Was it coincidental that the subject had been much on his mind since he had updated his will? He had no child to pass his wealth on to but there were good causes and not all of them were females with a taste for designer shoes.

As he had left the lawyer's office the older man had shaken his hand warmly and said with a smile, 'No doubt the next time we see you will be when you marry or have your first child?'

Roman prided himself on focusing his energy on things he could change, not lost causes. Anyone who got to be thirty and didn't realise that life was not fair was either very stupid or very lucky. He was neither, so he had not wasted time bewailing the hand fate had dealt him. He got on with life—a life that would not contain a family. He'd thought he had come to terms with it, but now…?

Had he only been seeing in Lily what he wanted to see? he wondered. Did he imagine the resemblance the child had to his family line? No, he dismissed the possibility almost immediately.

After his parents' deaths he had discovered a box of photographs and one among the dozens of images had been of him on his first birthday. The likeness between that image and Lily was not just striking, it was almost identical.

He'd had sex with her mother and now two years later his mystery woman turned up with a baby who looked impossibly like him. It did not take a genius to do the maths…

'Michelle said that Lily was fourteen months old, but she must be nearly fifteen months…?'

'Fourteen, she was premature.' The long labour had ended in an emergency Caesarean when the baby had become distressed.

The silence stretched between them, broken finally by Roman's hoarse voice. 'Were you ever going to tell me?' He could feel the vibration of a dull roar in his ears as his stunned gaze narrowed and swung her way. She'd had ample opportunity to come clean and she hadn't.

Izzy registered the accusation in his glare and let out a grunt of sheer disbelief. How dared he act like some innocent victim? Presumably he had conveniently absolved himself of all responsibility!

'Telling you was never an option—I didn't know your name.' Hard not to say it out loud without feeling shame.

'You were the one who insisted on anonymity,' he reminded her grimly. She was not the one who had encouraged him to have unprotected sex, though, reminded the voice in his head. In his defence, in a brief moment of sanity he had made an attempt to ask her if she was protected, but it had been an attempt he'd abandoned when she had touched a finger to his lips, encouraging him to be silent. 'And I meant today, or didn't you recognise the father of your child?'

Oh, yeah, because there was more than one man out there that looked like him.

'Oh, so now it's *my* child…' She smiled and had the satisfaction of seeing his jaw clench. 'Make your mind up, Roman.' His flush suggested she had made her point.

'And when was I meant to tell you about her? In the middle of the marriage service perhaps? Or during our delightful walk back here?' she snapped. 'It was kind of hard to get a word in edgewise while you were so charmingly propositioning me. Tell me, does the *I need you* line normally work for you? *I want you, really*?'

'It worked with you. No, I take that back, you were the one that said that, weren't you?'

The seamless comeback sent a flush of shame to Izzy's pale face. 'Look, I know this was a shock for you and I'm trying to make allowances—'

'That's really good of you,' he said in a voice like dry ice.

'Well, one of us has to act like an adult!' she snapped back.

'I'm struggling here, but what exactly is adult about hiding from me?' he drawled sarcastically.

She cast a quick furtive glance over her shoulder. They were alone but for the pianist and the dozing guest, but that situation could not last. 'Yes, I was avoiding you, because I didn't want this sort of public scene. I just knew you'd react like this...' She stopped, the anger fading from her face as she finished. 'Actually I didn't have a clue how you'd react. For all I knew you'd prefer to ignore Lily's existence.'

'And that would have suited you?' He watched the way her expression changed as she glanced towards the happily playing tot, the slow smile that transformed her face.

Izzy hesitated. This was a subject where her opinions were still lurching dramatically from one side of the argument to the other. She voiced the one thing she was sure of, though he might not agree. 'It would have been your loss.'

Roman could not argue with this assessment and quite suddenly he felt his anger towards her dissipate. He was blaming her for something that was not a curse, but a blessing.

'I'm a father... *Madre di Dio...*!' It shouldn't

be possible but it was. Roman felt a fresh explosion of wonder but it still didn't fully sink in. 'Did you try and find me?'

'How could I? Where would I have started?' He took a step closer, a tall and overpoweringly male presence that made her feel trapped. She lifted a hand to her throat to cover the pulse she could feel beating there.

'Do I make you nervous, Isabel?' He stepped closer again, his nostrils flaring as the scent of her perfume brought back memories his body responded to hungrily, making him uncomfortably aware of the heaviness in his groin. 'Isabel. I like that name, it suits you…'

His husky voice sent a secret shiver down her spine. Her pale skin was dusted with a layer of perspiration from the effort of concealing her emotional turmoil. 'Not Isabel, Izzy. People call me Izzy.'

'I'm not people.' *I'm the father of your child.*

His facial muscles froze as he fought an internal battle to regain control of his feelings. He focused on the positive: his child would not grow up not knowing he existed.

The sheer breathtaking arrogance of this pronouncement made Izzy blink, and yet it was hardly surprising if he had such a high opinion of himself.

Her eyes drifted over the carved contours of his chiselled cheek to his sensually sculpted mouth and the mole just visible in the carved contours of his cheek. She expelled a long shaky sigh. He was the most handsome man she had ever seen. His charismatic sex appeal was off the scale and his amazing looks must have always made him the focus of attention in any room he occupied.

CHAPTER FOUR

'FOR the record, I'm really not the nervous type.' But Izzy was the type to find Roman's sexual aura of masculinity totally overwhelming. Though that could hardly make her unique; his sexual charisma meant that every woman in the room stared at him.

He had been the one asking the questions but there was one that was troubling Izzy.

'Were you…are you married?'

'It's a bit late to develop a moral conscience.'

She narrowed her eyes. 'Were you?'

'I've never been married, but I had a close shave.'

She was relieved. At least that was one thing she didn't have to feel guilty about, though more from luck than good judgement.

'You got cold feet?' She didn't blame him. The

idea of committing to one person for the rest of your life was a scary thought.

He gave a sardonic smile. 'No, I got dumped.'

She waited for the punchline. When it didn't come her eyes widened. 'You're not serious!'

'How good you are for my ego,' he drawled. 'However, not everyone finds me as irresistible as you do.'

His ego was titanium coated, she was sure.

Responding to the tug on her skirt, Izzy bent down and picked up Lily.

'She is a pretty baby.' He softened his voice and said, 'Hello, Lily.'

Responding to her name, Lily reached out, her chubby fingers closing around his pale grey silk tie. Chuckling, she pulled and Roman didn't resist. His face came in close, so close that Izzy could see the fine-pored texture of his skin, the gold tips to his long sooty lashes…smell the cologne that elicited a rush of memories.

'I'm sorry,' Izzy muttered, her face flaming as she tried to unpeel her daughter's fingers from the fabric. She was unable to stop her eyes sliding sideways to his taut aquiline profile and her quiet desperation grew.

Roman could see the stress in the skin stretched tight across the fine bone structure of her face, but felt little sympathy. 'That's something, I suppose.'

Izzy pretended not to hear the muttered comment as her breast brushed his arm. This was not the time or place for any sort of confrontation and she had enough on her plate coping with being this close to him. The scent of his lean, hard body continued to trigger all sorts of memories that she had imagined she had deleted. Heat travelled in a wave over the surface of her skin, causing the silk of her bodice to cling to her damp skin.

'She looks like me.'

Breathing far too hard, actually panting, Izzy gave a grunt of relief as Lily loosened her grip and she took a step backwards. 'At least she missed out on the freckles,' she said, directing her gaze at his crumpled tie.

His hooded gaze moved upwards in a long assessing sweep from her feet and stilled on her face. He felt the kick of desire in his belly and for a moment the strength of the raw physical attraction swamped the anger and resentment he was containing. Barely.

'She's beautiful.'

Normally when anyone commented on her baby's remarkable beauty Izzy glowed with pride. On this occasion she stiffened. 'I know.'

In the periphery of her vision she was aware of a group of laughing guests entering the room, their chatter drowning out that of the pianist playing in the corner. She felt a stab of relief, as Roman surely wouldn't continue this conversation in the middle of a crowd…would he?

She didn't have a clue.

He might be the father of her child, but she didn't know him at all and she had no idea what he was capable of, at least outside the bedroom. The mental addition caused a memory to surface and desire to pound through her blood, pooling hot and achy in her pelvis.

'She looks like you.'

'I have been called many things, but not beautiful.'

If that was true then she was amazed, because he was the epitome of male beauty.

'Is she a happy baby?'

Izzy glimpsed a yearning in his face as he stared at Lily that made her look away quickly, feeling like an intruder.

So far she hadn't spent much time wondering how he was feeling. Anger and suspicion would both be natural responses for a man who realised he had fathered a baby, but was he resenting being landed with a responsibility that he hadn't planned or asked for?

'Look, I know we need to talk, but not here... *please.*'

For a moment she thought he was going to refuse her request, then he nodded and she felt a rush of relief. 'I'm not staying here. I'm in the Fox—do you know it?'

Izzy nodded. The new manager who had been recruited by the boutique hotel had been asking her out on a weekly basis since she'd dined there weeks before. Izzy had not accepted his offer, though she hadn't ruled out the possibility she would in the future. She liked him and, as Emma said, being a mum was not the same as being a nun.

'I know it.'

'I'm in the garden suite. Meet me there at...' his eyes narrowed as he did some mental calculation '...eight tonight.'

Her reaction to the order wrapped up as an invitation was immediate. 'I'm not coming to your room.' She intercepted his look and, lifting her chin, added, 'I'd prefer somewhere more public.'

'I'm not trying to get you into bed.' When was a fling not a fling? He now knew the answer: when it was with the mother of your child.

Izzy matched his sarcasm. 'Imagine my disappointment.'

'Bring the baby if that makes you feel any better,' he suggested, sounding bored.

'I can't. She'll be in bed.'

Roman clenched his jaw. She might be being deliberately obstructive or she might be stating the truth. With his zero knowledge of child care he was in no position to judge. 'All right. Tomorrow morning.'

He watched as she licked her lips and ran the tip of her tongue across the soft plump contours before catching the full lower lip between her white teeth and chewing. She nodded and his heavy eyelids drooped partially, concealing the gleam that had lit them.

'Nine-thirty?' he said, still staring at her mouth. Tomorrow when he'd had time to calm down and get things straight in his head might be better, he told himself. *Who are you fooling...?* It would take a hell of a lot longer to get anything straight. Finding himself face to face with a child who was unmistakeably his had been the most shocking experience of his life, which in itself was quite shocking considering this was a man who had sat in a doctor's office and been given a fifty-fifty chance of surviving to his next birthday.

'The park that the hotel backs onto, I walk there with—' Izzy broke off, bending her head as she winced and began to free the strands from the tenacious little fingers that had grabbed her hair. 'No, Lily, that hurts.'

The baby ignored the plea, seemingly fascinated by the glossy mesh of her mother's hair as she sank her chubby fingers deeper. Roman could identify with the fascination. He could remember burying his face in the soft, sweet-smelling chestnut waves, feeling them whisper across his chest and belly as she'd slid down his body. He inhaled and pushed the thought away, but not before his body had hardened helplessly in response to the image. 'Let me...' he husked.

'No!' She jerked her head back, causing her eyes to fill with tears of pain as her daughter's little hand came free with several strands of her hair.

Roman's hand fell away in a gesture of exaggerated surrender. 'Anyone would think you're afraid of me.' The idea bothered him more than a little.

Her chin tilted an extra defiant inch. 'I'm not afraid of you.' More afraid, quite irrationally, of herself. Crazy! It wasn't as if his touch were

going to turn her into some wild, wanton creature with a moral compass wildly out of whack.

He'd kissed her and she had walked away.
Round of applause, Izzy.

'Just one thing I need to know.' He hadn't intended to ask, but it was out there now and a man
had a right to know if he'd been used.

'Did you do it on purpose?'

She looked at him, her blue eyes narrowed, her
smooth brow creased in furrows of incomprehen-
sion. 'Do what?'

'Get pregnant,' he said bluntly.

The possibility had not occurred to him until
the wedding breakfast, when he had been seated
at a table with his old friend Gianni Fitzgerald
and his lovely wife. Roman had struggled to tune
out the slightly tipsy woman sitting opposite him
without being outright rude and her anecdotes
had become more scurrilous as the interminable
meal had gone on.

He had managed tolerably well until he'd heard
the name of Michael Fitzgerald's older daughter

mentioned and after that he had unashamedly egged the woman on.

'Of course, Michael was young and this woman was a real man hater. She never told him she wanted a baby...planned it all in cold blood.' The woman, speaking behind her hand, had paused for dramatic effect or possibly to catch her breath before continuing. 'But it's Michelle I feel sorry for. Of course, she puts on a brave face, but to have the girl living in the village! And now there's the baby and no father, it makes you think, maybe it's a family tradition...?'

Her laugh had been cut off when Gianni had at this point picked up on the conversation and intervened, closing down his garrulous relative smoothly, but not before the seed of suspicion had been planted in Roman's brain.

The blood drained from Izzy's face as his meaning sank in. She gave a shrug, choking back the anger and glancing over her shoulder to make sure their conversation wasn't being overheard.

'For the record, no, I did *not* plan to get pregnant. And if I had been looking for a perfect genetic specimen to father my child I would not,' she gritted through clenched teeth, 'have chosen one who thinks he's God's gift…an arrogant, humourless, bossy idiot who—'

'You have forgotten the limp,' he drawled, cutting off her diatribe.

Izzy threw up her hands in angry exasperation. 'I don't give a damn about your limp.' And neither did any woman she had seen today, she thought, recalling the lustful female stares that seemed to follow his progress. 'But I wouldn't deliberately lumber my kid with a dad as stupid as you are. I always thought that when I had a child it would be with someone who—'

She took a deep breath and, aware of the curious glances their impassioned exchange was receiving, she lowered her voice to a husky murmur and added, 'I didn't plan anything. I was…' Her eyes fell. 'I don't normally…'

'Jump into bed with a total stranger?'

The interjection brought a flush of shamed anger to her cheeks. 'I really don't think you're in any position to occupy the moral high ground…

or is it different for men?' she snipped back sarcastically.

His face darkened with annoyance. 'This is not about blame.'

She elevated a delicate brow. 'Just as well, because from where I'm standing you don't come off very white-knight-on-a-charger in all this.'

Roman watched her walk away, the child in her arms, her narrow back straight and proud. She was right: he was in no position to throw stones; his behaviour had been totally indefensible. So he had genuinely believed that there was no chance of him getting her pregnant, but, unwanted pregnancies aside, unprotected sex with a stranger made him criminally stupid.

It made him the man he had always despised. Someone so selfish he was unable to think about anything beyond his own pleasure.

CHAPTER FIVE

FOR the sake of her sanity, when Izzy left the reception she blocked everything out and tried to think of nothing beyond a quiet night at home with Lily. She had to try and regroup and get her head back together. Tomorrow would be time enough to worry about what she was going to say to Roman Petrelli.

That was the plan, but as with most best laid plans it went sadly awry.

Izzy's went wrong in a major way the moment she opened the door of her cottage and found Michelle and her father standing there.

'I had to tell him,' Michelle said.

Izzy sighed. 'Of course.'

It was after midnight before they left and at least by the time they had left her father was no longer planning to confront Roman Petrelli.

Izzy was touched that he wanted to protect her but she struggled with the idea of anyone fighting her battles for her, having always been taught not to rely on anyone but herself.

On the other hand she had been grateful for the help her father had provided when Lily had been born. It had been Michael who had suggested she stay permanently in Cumbria with them—after all they were her family.

Izzy had been touched by the offer, but she could think of no surer way to destroy the delicate new relationship she had found with her new family than imposing herself on them with her new baby. Besides, Izzy needed her own space too.

It had been Michelle who had come up with the compromise that they could all live with, and Izzy had moved into the cottage on the edge of the village a mile or so from the family farmhouse where her half-brother and -sister had spent their childhoods.

It was hard sometimes not to contrast their lives with her own. Her mother had taught her some valuable things like independence and self-reliance, but had not taught her about casual physical demonstrations of affection or the teasing that went with life in a close-knit family group.

But despite the acceptance of the family Izzy still felt an outsider at times. Not because they excluded her, but because she recognised a need to maintain her own distance.

But living in the cottage she was close enough to enjoy the support of her new family and far enough away to maintain her independence, and it gave everyone the space they needed.

After her father and Michelle had finally gone Izzy went to bed herself, but she slept badly. But it wasn't a hunting owl or a fox that had kept her awake or even the darkness. It was the thought of meeting Roman Petrelli this morning.

Lily, normally a fairly sunny baby, seemed to have picked up on her mother's mood and was cranky this morning too. She had taken hours to eat her breakfast and had fought every step of the way Izzy's attempts to dress her. By the time she was finally ready to leave, a good ten minutes later than planned, Izzy felt drained.

Glancing in the hall mirror, she saw that she looked even worse than she felt, with violet smudges darkening the underneath of her eyes.

Izzy was tempted to dash back inside to at least apply some blusher to alleviate her sleep-deprived pallor and give her confidence a bit of a boost, but she had no time. Instead she manufactured a smile for her reflection and reminded herself that Roman probably wouldn't notice her less than yummy-mummy appearance and so what? She wasn't out to impress him anyway.

A brisk walk up the hill meant she wasn't pale when she arrived at the hotel, her cheeks flushed with the exertion of pushing the buggy.

As she struggled to push it across the gravel forecourt a tall figure emerged from the side of the building. Unlike yesterday she was prepared for his appearance, but even so her heart started pounding like a hammer and her knees started to tremble.

'I'm sorry I'm late.' The breathless quiver

was, she told herself, nothing to do with the fact that he radiated an aura of raw masculinity—he really was breathtaking!

'No matter.' His dark glance slid to the sleeping child and he tried to analyse the emotions that tightened like a fist in his chest. Once he had taken having a child for granted. Now it seemed more miracle.

'Would you like a coffee?'

'Actually it might be a good idea to walk and talk. Lily will wake up if I stop pushing her and she's quite cranky this morning.'

They did walk but there was no talk.

She endured the silent attrition for ten minutes, during which time her apprehension had increased tenfold until she could bear it no more.

They had reached the footpath that circled the lake when Izzy had had enough. 'Let's sit, shall we?'

Roman tilted his head. 'Fine.' With one hand in the small of her back he guided her towards one of the benches beside the lake.

Izzy sat down, resisting the impulse that made

her want to shuffle to the far end when Roman sat down beside her. He was a man with an overpowering presence and the sort of sexual charisma she had thought was an invention of romantic fiction.

He took a bag out of the pocket of his long black trench coat and tipped the contents on the ground, giving an awkward grimace when he caught her astonished stare. 'I bought some food for the ducks. I thought Lily might like...?' He nodded to the sleeping child.

'That's very thoughtful of you,' she said. 'She's tired...and it's probably easier to talk without...'

She stopped and raised her voice above the squawks of the ducks who had mobbed them. 'I have to be back by twelve. Emma is picking Lily up. She goes back to university tomorrow and she wants to spend some time with her.' Her half-sister was a doting aunt.

A nerve clenched in Roman's lean cheek as he turned to look at her. 'So do I.'

His direct stare brought a flush to her cheeks. 'Oh, of course...I didn't think...'

'She's my daughter.' If he said it out loud often enough it might start to feel more real.

Izzy nodded tightly.

Roman swallowed and dug his fingers deep into the dark pelt of hair on his head.

'I appreciate all this must be a shock for you.'

Roman's hand fell away, leaving his sleek hair standing up in spiky tufts on his scalp. 'Shock!' He gave a twisted smile and laughed. 'You have no idea.' He stretched out his long legs in front of him and loosened the button on his coat, the fabric parting to reveal the dark cashmere sweater he wore underneath.

Izzy felt the muscles in her stomach quiver. He really was an extraordinarily attractive man.

'I thought Lily was a grumbling appendix until I was six months pregnant.'

Her attempt to inject a note of levity—good timing never had been her strong point—was greeted with an incredulous stare. 'Seriously?'

'No, not seriously.' She had known immediately, even before she'd done the test. She had simply felt different.

He turned his head. 'I never thought I'd have a child.' He still struggled to get his head around the idea.

So children did not figure in the glamorous life of this man. No real surprise there—it was hard to imagine him welcoming grubby fingerprints on his shirt.

'I suppose not everyone likes children.'

She felt herself relax slightly. Was that what this meeting was about—a warning to tell her not to expect him to be a hands-on parent? He needn't have worried; she didn't need or want anything from him. As far as she was concerned her daughter had all the positive male role models she needed.

'I'll let you know how Lily is, a yearly update if you like.' He was looking at her oddly so she shrugged and added, 'Or not.' Then looked away because those spooky silver lights deep in his dark eyes made her feel dizzy.

Had she assumed too much? Did he want to walk away and act as though nothing had happened?

'Though it would be useful to know if there is any significant medical history on your side…?' This practicality was the reason her mother had decided to give her the details of her biological father, in case after she was gone Izzy found herself in a situation where such information would be useful.

His thick, strongly defined sable brows knitted together as he stared at her as though she were talking gibberish. 'I didn't say I didn't like children. Actually I don't know any.'

Unlike the large and noisy Fitzgerald clan, he had been an only child and there had been no cousins to play with. His parents, madly in love and totally wrapped up in one another, had never intended to have children, and resented the intrusion of a third party, and at an early age Roman had been shipped off to school. He hadn't minded. He'd liked school, excelling academically and at sports, though not team sports—Roman with his lone-wolf tendencies had never been a team player.

'Though I was one myself once,' he added with a half-smile.

'You don't have brothers or sisters...?' Izzy asked and he shook his head. 'Neither do I, but then I'm sure the grapevine gossip told you that.'

Instead of reacting to the charge he picked up on the previous statement. 'Actually I was told that I couldn't have children, or at any rate it would be unlikely.'

But unlikely had happened, a miracle had happened. Did she really think he'd be content with yearly updates on his child's life?

Izzy was confused by his admission. She knew he was not impotent so that left what...?

'Three years ago I had chemo.' He offered the additional information in the manner of a casual afterthought.

Her eyes flew to his face 'You're ill?' Beneath the calm surface Izzy could feel the ice forming...counting, she waited for the next breath. 'You're not dying? God, no!' She took a deep breath, let it out in a long hissing sigh and made a struggling attempt to breach the social chasm that had opened up at her feet.

His broad shoulders lifted in a fluid shrug. 'We are all dying, *cara.*'

Izzy, conscious that her knees were shaking, flashed him a dark look, annoyed that he was making light of a subject that was anything but. 'You know what I mean.'

He conceded the point. 'I had the all-clear, but surgery…well, you saw the scars.'

He watched as she closed her eyes, her long curling lashes fluttering like butterfly wings. Her eyelids lifted. 'Well, you might have said that straight off instead…'

'Sorry.'

Two years ago he had been in remission and the doctors had been cautiously optimistic, explaining that if he went another two years then his chances of suffering the disease were no more than those of any other member of the population. If it did return then worst-case scenario would be to amputate the leg.

Roman touched his leg now at the thought. The

metal inserted to replace the diseased section might give him pain and preclude him enjoying some of the athletic pursuits he once had, but it was a hell of a lot better than the alternative!

He had cheated death, but for a while it could just have easily gone the other way. Life was that fragile. Not that he had dwelt on the possibility of death for long. What would have been the point? Such things were out of his hands and if he had learnt anything from the experience it was not to waste time worrying about things over which you had no control.

Izzy released the breath she had not been aware of holding. 'You were awfully young for...'

'Cancer? Yes, I was twenty-eight.'

God, so young at a time when a man like Roman would think he was invincible. 'But they must have...I mean, don't they...freeze your...?'

'Are my future children in a test tube in some laboratory somewhere?' His eyes flashed as she blushed and nodded.

'Yes, but due to a technical glitch they got thawed prematurely.'

Her eyes widened. 'That's terrible! You said you were dumped. Is that why…?'

'The beautiful Lauren gave me back my ring? Actually she kept the ring, but, no, she was fine with the idea of a baby-free life. Unfortunately, I made the mistake of admitting to her that if the cancer returned then there was the possibility that they might have to amputate my leg. Poor Lauren couldn't stand the idea of being stuck with a cripple.'

Izzy's contempt for this woman knew no bounds.

'She sounds like a total and complete idiot!' she fumed, wondering if underneath the cynical, amused façade he wasn't still in love with this prize bitch.

Probably—men had no judgement when it came to beautiful women.

She caught him looking at her oddly and added quickly, 'I'd have thought they'd have had all sorts of backups to prevent that kind of thing from happening?'

'They do, but they also have human error.' The

sympathy in her wide clear eyes was genuine, as was the dismay when he added, 'Lily might be my one chance to be a father and I intend to be fully involved in her life.'

Fully involved. The words made her uncomfortable. 'I get that…I see, but I'm sure you'll have your own family.'

'I already have a family.'

'We're not…' Izzy took a deep breath and forced herself to speak more moderately. 'In what way, fully?' she asked, struggling not to sound defensive and knowing she hadn't succeeded.

Roman held her eyes and set out his intentions so that there was no chance of her misunderstanding. 'In every way…'

He saw her blue eyes flicker and the muscles beneath the pale skin of her throat ripple as she swallowed, probably wondering what he knew about being a father. But what did he know about being a father?

Refusing to acknowledge the rare voice of silent self-doubt, Roman pushed it away.

'I hope you'll help me.' Roman felt he was

being pretty fair given the circumstances, but he would learn with or without her help. 'I've already missed out on the first months of her life.' Roman stifled the resentment that made the muscle in his cheek clench. What was important, he reminded himself, was the future.

'And for that you blame me.'

'I'm trying hard not to.' But her attitude was making it increasingly difficult; she was so spiky and damned confrontational.

Sensitive to the thread of accusation in his voice, Izzy raised her chin. She was perfectly willing to take responsibility for her part. She'd had sex with a stranger and had got pregnant— not something she was proud of—but she hadn't done so alone.

'I realise it might be difficult for you to share Lily…'

Her eyes widened and she shifted uncomfortably in her seat. Holding the buggy handle, she used her free hand to lift the collar of her jacket against the chill breeze that was blowing.

'And why the name Lily?' Roman asked, looking at the sleeping child.

'Why. Don't you like it?'

The suggestion of a smile vanished from his sensual lips as he turned his attention back to Izzy. 'Do you have to be so defensive? Look, if you want a fight I can do that,' he said, now visibly exasperated.

'Of course I don't.'

'Actually, I like the name…' A name he had had no part in choosing. He pushed away the thought and the anger that came with it.

'Roman, I would have told you about her, but I had no idea how to contact you.' She gave a laugh to hide her embarrassment and managed to inject a note of rueful amusement into her voice as she added, 'I didn't even know your name.'

'You could have hung around to find out.'

'When I woke up you were gone.' Izzy closed her eyes, feeling the familiar sick churning of shame and self-disgust in her stomach as she relived the moment she'd realised that her lover of the previous night had not waited for her to wake up.

That had been the grim reality for her in the early hours of the morning after she had fallen asleep in the arms of her lover, believing this was perhaps the start of a love affair between two people destined to be together.

Even the memory embarrassed her now.

Now she knew it had just been sex. Casual sex.

'I'd only gone across the road to...' Izzy shrugged and lowered her gaze, still able to recall the guilt and self-disgust she had felt when she had woken up in that strange room alone. She intended never to forget it.

'It doesn't matter now, Roman. It was such a long time ago.'

'And you have so many meaningless affairs that you might have me mixed up with someone else?'

'Hardly an affair,' she countered calmly. 'More a one-night stand.'

'I have no taste for semantics.'

'Well, I like things to be clear...and clearly I'm not your family.'

'You're the mother of my child. That makes you my family.'

Izzy's teeth clenched in frustration as she watched his dark eyes follow a young woman wheeling a pushchair along a path that ran parallel to the lake. She released a hissing sigh and dragged a hand down her cheek, tucking the stray shiny strands of hair behind her ear.

'You can visit Lily any time you like.'

'I don't want to visit Lily.' His dark eyes held hers as he dropped the bombshell so casually that she barely heard it go off. 'I want to watch her grow up. I want to help her with her homework. I don't want to visit her—I want to live with her. Support her...'

'I support her. I've been supporting her for the past fourteen months.'

'How?'

His scepticism irritated the hell out of her.

'What do you want—a report? A letter from my bank manager or my CV?' She gave a snort at his expression.

'You work? You're an academic like your mother?'

'No, I'm not an academic.'

His brow lifted. 'Have I touched a nerve?'

'No, you have not touched a nerve!' she yelled, then, encountering the ironic glitter in his eyes, bit her lip. 'I did an interior design course at college and got a place with Urquarts.'

'Impressive. It must have been hard to leave.'

'How do you know I've left?'

'You are living in Cumbria,' he pointed out. 'Not really commutable distance.'

'Oh, yes…well, actually I've done a couple of small commissions the past few months on a self-employed basis… It's simply a matter of juggling.' Ten balls in the air but she wasn't about to admit to him how difficult it was.

'It is wise, no doubt, for you to keep your hand in, considering how hard it will be for you to get your feet back on the career ladder, but I'm sure you already know that.'

'It is possible to have a career and be a mother.'

'Of course it is.'

Her eyes narrowed. 'Are you patronising me?' she asked in a dangerous voice.

His dark brows lifted. 'I am admiring you. Clearly if you got a job with Urquarts you are good at what you do and ambitious...?'

Izzy responded to his quizzical look with a blank expression, determined not to give him any ammunition to use against her.

'It is good for a woman to be ambitious and stimulated by her work, but the balancing act will be much easier to achieve when you have support...when you are not living alone.'

Izzy just stared at him for a speechless moment. Had he heard a thing she had said? Finally shaking her head, she surged to her feet. 'That isn't going to happen. Lily lives with me...she needs me...I need her...no...no...no!'

She reminded him of a tigress defending her young as she positioned herself between him and the buggy. 'Calm down. I'm not trying to take Lily off you. There are ways around this.'

She folded her arms across her chest. 'Amaze me.'

'We both want to live with Lily, so the obvious solution would be to cohabit. Another option we should not discount out of hand, of course, is marriage…a definite possibility.'

Izzy stared at him and thought, *My God, he's insane! My baby's father is a lunatic. Marriage, he actually said marriage!*

'You're joking, right?'

'I'm deadly serious.'

Izzy grabbed the buggy. 'Just keep away from me and Lily.'

'You're being very emotional about this.'

'Too right,' she said, turning the buggy around.

He rose with a curse. 'Look, you're not letting me explain this properly. You're not going to deny that a child needs two parents.'

'Not if one of them is insane.'

'When I said marriage I was simply referring to a contractual arrangement, not a romantic one.'

'Love and marriage, now who ever heard of such a crazy idea? It'll never catch on.'

'I'm thinking of Lily. Who are you thinking of?' he yelled after her, smiling despite himself when without turning she made a rude gesture over her shoulder.

'I'll be back!'

She did turn then, yelling, 'I've heard it before and the other guy was much more impressive.'

CHAPTER SIX

THE only person Izzy had confided in was Michelle, whom she described the conversation to over coffee and cakes the next morning.

She laughed about it and made it sound like a joke but in truth she was really anxious. Would he try and take Lily from her?

Then Michelle reacted in a way Izzy had never anticipated and instead of condemning Roman she actually defended him.

'Well, I'm not saying it wasn't over the top, but at least he isn't trying to dodge his responsibilities, which a lot of men in this situation would, you know. Did he actually propose? It's actually rather romantic when you think about it...'

'Well, not actually propose in so many words,' Izzy admitted. 'And believe me, it *wasn't* romantic.'

'So has he been in touch since yesterday?'

'No, and he's booked out of the Fox.' Izzy hoped she had seen the last of Roman Petrelli… didn't she?

Later that day Izzy was interrupted from her power walking back home by her phone ringing. Chest heaving, she stopped to pull the phone from her pocket halfway up the steep country lane. The calm objectivity she was trying to exhaust herself into still eluded her.

Roman's *I'll be back* threat still haunted her.

It was all about what he wanted, and, yes, today he wanted to be a father, but what did he know about being a parent? Nothing, he had said as much himself, and would he be equally enthusiastic when the novelty of the situation wore off?

'Yes!' she breathed into the phone.

'Izzy, is that you?' Layla, the owner of the interior design agency she had worked for straight from college, sounded startled…and small wonder.

Izzy took a deep breath. 'Yes, Layla…sorry, I was just…'

Layla as always got straight to the point. 'I've got a job for you, a big job. It's perfect, it's… I've got it down somewhere, but it's in the middle of the country—you like the country, darling.'

'That sounds great, Layla, and I appreciate you thinking of me, but until Lily is older and at school it's difficult. The commission in Keswick last month was great, but anything bigger…?' The older woman had continued to put some part-time commissions her way and Izzy was grateful.

'Oh, I didn't think about you, darling—the client specifically requested you.'

'Me?'

'Seems like he saw the Dublin town-house project you worked on before Lily was born— did you know it was on the market? Anyhow, apparently he was blown away.'

Izzy felt a stab of pride. She had been pretty pleased with the project herself. 'So the client is Irish?'

'Not a clue, darling.'

Izzy frowned and glared at the nail she had just caught herself nibbling before thrusting her hand in her pocket. 'So you don't actually know who this client is?'

'What does that matter? A film star, a royal, an oil-rich sheikh—he won't be there. Apparently there's just a skeleton staff. The point is he's got pots of money, expense is no object and he'll give you a free hand.'

'Free hand? There must be a remit?'

'Nope. He's apparently willing to put himself entirely in your hands. The only stipulation is that it is a suitable family home to take his bride to…lucky girl. Oh, yes, it is a he.'

'It sounds too good to be true…' Izzy found herself almost hoping that there would be a catch; it would make it easier to justify refusing it.

It wasn't that she regretted her decision to take a career break, but the sense of guilt she felt lingered.

Her own mother had worked up until the day before Izzy's birth and had returned to work two weeks after. She had always encouraged ambition in her daughter and instilled the importance of having a career and being independent, and she would have been appalled that Izzy had taken even a temporary career break to look after her baby.

Ironically it was thanks to her mother that Izzy was financially able to take time off at all to spend with Lily. Izzy was still receiving healthy royalties cheques from her mother's successful writing career.

'A gig like this could make your career, Izzy.'

'True.' And two years ago Izzy would have jumped at the golden opportunity. 'And I appreciate the offer, but the timing's not right,' she said firmly.

'Is this about leaving Lily? Because, you know, you don't have to. Part of the remit is to make the place child friendly, not just a show house— a family home. Lily could be your guinea pig!'

'Really?' Izzy's thoughts raced. That did put a different slant on it.

'I'd say go and think it over but the only problem is—'

'I knew this was too good to be true.'

'They want you to start immediately.'

'How immediately?'

'Right away…as in tomorrow.'

Izzy was shaking her head. Organising Lily for a trip to the local supermarket took her an hour. 'Well, that's just not…' She stopped, an arrested expression stealing across her face as she thought, *What am I doing?*

Suddenly she felt her excitement growing. Far from being bad timing, this could actually be perfect timing! 'Tomorrow?'

'You'll take it…' The relief in the older woman's voice was unmistakeable.

'Where is this place?'

'Oh, you won't need directions,' Layla replied when Izzy asked for the address and a contact number. 'There will be a car to pick you up at the station. It couldn't be simpler. Just let me know what train you'll be on and I'll pass on the details. And don't forget to keep your receipts. The client is willing to pay all travel expenses and I didn't even have to ask.'

* * *

Simple—if she didn't already know that Layla was childless this phrase would have cleared up any confusion, Izzy decided as she disembarked from the train with a baby buggy and her baggage.

She felt hot and sticky as Lily's beaker of juice had spilled down her linen trousers. On the plus side the stain distracted from the creases in her trousers and she decided that linen had perhaps not been the best choice. But she had wanted to make a good first impression and the wide-legged trousers teamed with her favourite silk shirt had seemed to say professional competence. Ah, well, fingers crossed her new client was not someone who judged by appearances.

It wasn't until she exited the railway station that it occurred to Izzy she had no idea where she was going, let alone who was picking her up. A situation a normal person could be relaxed about, but not one with a baby.

As she manoeuvred the buggy laden with bags she saw a silver four-wheel drive taking up sev-

eral parking spaces. As she approached the door
opened and a man wearing a dark suit got out
from the massive car with blacked-out windows.

The man did not hesitate, but approached her
directly. 'Miss Fitzgerald?'

Her brows rose. She hadn't been expecting the
strong Italian accent. 'Yes, that's me.' She tipped
her head in acknowledgement and nodded, regis-
tering the width of his shoulders. 'How did you
know?'

The man removed his dark glasses and shot out
a hand to stop the holdall balanced on top of her
case from falling to the ground.

'The boss described you.'

Presumably a woman with a baby.

'Here, I've got it,' he added, taking the buggy
she had lifted Lily from and snapping it closed
with an expert action.

'You look like an expert, Mr...?'

'Gennaro, miss, just Gennaro. Grandchildren,'
he added by way of explanation.

'Hello, Gennaro, and thank you,' she added as
he tossed the heavier of her suitcases into the

boot space beside the buggy with impressive ease. Those shoulders were not just for show, it seemed.

He flashed her what she presumed passed as a smile in his world, but might have been a grimace. The man had a face that made a granite rock face look expressive.

'Is it far?' Izzy asked as she settled herself in the back seat. Lily was strapped securely into a baby seat beside her, her lavishly lashed eyes already closing.

The driver glanced at her in the rear-view mirror. His shades were back in place. 'No.'

Izzy didn't press him for more information, partly because he was negotiating rush-hour traffic through a busy market town and partly because he did not look a man who wanted to chat. She leaned back in her seat and decided to enjoy the journey.

Once they had left the town behind the countryside in this area proved pretty. As she gazed at the passing scenery her thoughts began to wander into territory she had been avoiding.

Would Roman have fulfilled his threat of 'I'll be back'—expecting her to give ground? What would he do when he discovered she was gone?

The thoughts going through her mind made Izzy frown. She chewed her lip and tried to summon some of the defiant certainty that she had begun the journey with.

Relax, she told herself. *This is the right thing to do.* Annoyed that she felt the need to justify her actions, she shook her head and with a spurt of defiance said out loud, 'What could he do?'

Embarrassed, she looked around. Lily was still sleeping, her face flushed, and the driver gave no hint of having heard her, concentrating hard on the road ahead.

Izzy lowered her rigid body back into the leather seat, not realising until that moment how knotted the muscles in her neck and spine were.

Your trouble, Izzy, she told herself, *is that you worry too much and have a tendency to over-analyse.*

She had taken a job, not made a life-changing decision! True, she would feel better about it if her father and Michelle had not expressed their concerns over her decision to take the job, or at least the timing.

They had reluctantly agreed to her request not to give Roman any information about her whereabouts if he asked. In retrospect she could see that it was unfair of her to put them in that position. This was her problem, not theirs.

As her mum would have said, *Your mess, Izzy, you clean it up.* And she'd have been right.

Izzy exhaled a long gusty sigh, finally acknowledging the voice in the back of her mind she'd been trying very hard not to hear all day. When she rang the farm this evening to give them the address as promised, Izzy decided she would tell them they didn't have to lie for her. She leaned back in her seat, feeling some of the tension leave her shoulder blades. She felt a lot better having made that decision.

She would contact Roman herself and explain the situation. She recognised the real risk he'd come rushing down here throwing around his ultimatums and trying to take over her life, but it was one she felt she had to take. He did have a right to know where his daughter was.

She chewed her lip, fretfully gnawing at the soft flesh. Running away from her problems was just so not her. It made her seem…spineless, but the timing of the perfect job offer when she had been feeling so cornered by Roman had been too much of a temptation.

Well, the job was still perfect and on the plus side it might make Roman see her in a different light. This was an opportunity to show him she could have a career and be a good mother, that the two were not mutually exclusive. She needed to establish from the outset that she wasn't someone he could push around.

Izzy spent the next fifteen minutes of the journey working out what she would say to him, mentally rewriting and editing the conversation in her head, anticipating all his comments and coming up with some killer comebacks. By the time the car pulled off the highway and onto a long straight driveway lined with copper beeches she was confident that she had made her argument forcibly but in a calm, reasonable way.

And she would not make the mistake of apologising. Roman was the sort of man who equated apology with weakness. She had a perfect right to take a job without consulting him and she would make that quite clear.

As they reached the rise in the drive she leaned forward, looking through the windscreen anticipating seeing a house, but the drive just stretched on bounded either side by parkland grazed by sheep and a few cattle. 'Are we here?'

'Next bend you'll see it.'

Izzy sat up straighter in her seat, holding on to the door as the four-wheel drive negotiated a wooden bridge. 'Does all this land belong to the house? Oh, my goodness!'

'*Sì*, it is a bit of a dump,' came the dour response to her amazed gasp.

Izzy couldn't decide from his expression if he was joking or not because the dump he spoke of was an enormous golden-stoned mansion.

Izzy took a deep breath. 'It's beautiful.' Actually beautiful did not do the building justice; it was stunning, with mullioned windows and mellow golden stone—totally breathtaking!

Gennaro brought the car to a halt on the gravelled area in front of the house. 'The boss said—'

'Where is…?' Gennaro pulled open his door and she raised her voice, adding, 'When will I be meeting him and his wife?'

It was fine by her if the elusive clients did not want to be hands-on, but, as she had told Layla, it was essential that she at least meet them. Her job was not about ticking off a list of requirements or filling a place with the current fashionable must haves; a home had to reflect a person's personality.

'The boss isn't married—'

Izzy frowned as the man crunched around to her side. 'But I thought…' She accepted the hand he offered as she jumped down.

'And I'd say you're about to meet him.' In response to Izzy's questioning frown, he nodded his head to a point behind her. 'Here he is now. Don't worry about the baby. I'll get her out.'

Izzy turned around to face the direction the burly Italian indicated in time to see a tall, lithe figure vaulting over the six-bar gate that kept the sheep from straying into the garden.

'Oh, my God!' Izzy felt as if a giant hand had pushed into her chest and for several heart-thudding moments she literally couldn't breathe. *How do I get out of here?*

Roman, seemingly oblivious to her state of near collapse, walked straight up to the older man, who nodded and removed his shades. 'Any problems, Gennaro?'

'No, boss, the train was actually on time.' Gennaro unfastened the baby seat complete with baby and lifted it out.

'I'll take that.'

Izzy watched, too stunned to protest, as Roman took hold of the baby carrier.

'Should I take the bags up?'

'If you would. Oh, and could you ask Mrs Saunders to send some coffee through to the library, and maybe some sandwiches? Then I won't be needing either of you until tomorrow.'

Gennaro nodded his thanks at Roman and tacked something on the end of his conversation in Italian that made Roman laugh.

Izzy wasn't laughing.

She wasn't even capable of acknowledging Gennaro's nod as, with a case under each arm, he walked up the shallow flight of steps towards the open front door.

'Good trip, Isabel?'

He spoke as though this was a prearranged meeting, which of course it was—only she hadn't been kept in the loop. She had stepped right into the trap he'd so cleverly baited. He knew exactly what her weakness was; she'd told him about her guilt at being a stay-at-home mum even if she could afford it financially. And he had sown the seeds of doubt when he had suggested that it might not be so easy to step back into the job market after a lengthy break. This was the set-up to end all set-ups!

Why hadn't she seen it coming? The too-good-to-be-true offer…why hadn't she smelt a rat?

Possibly because she wasn't twisted and sneaky.

She wanted to laugh or throw something at him or both. Instead she stood like a rabbit caught in the headlights, thinking, *Any moment now I'll wake up and realise this was all a dream—a nightmare.*

'So what do you think?' he asked, gesturing towards the building behind them, but looking at Izzy.

She shivered at his voice. The dictionary would sound like an indecent proposal when read in that deep, husky, dangerously seductive timbre.

'This is your house.'

'I knew you'd get there eventually, *cara.*' He watched the two spots of angry colour appear on her smooth cheeks. 'So, what's your opinion… professionally speaking? Does it have potential?'

'Professionally?' she echoed, thinking very unprofessional thoughts as she fixed him with a murderous glare. Just how long was he going to insult her by pretending this job offer was anything but an elaborate hoax?

'I realise it's all subjective, but do you like the place? Could you see yourself—?'

'I can see myself pushing you off a cliff!'

She sucked in a deep breath, causing Roman's glance to drop. Having a baby changed a woman's body and though Izzy was lighter and more fragile-looking than he recalled, her breasts were definitely fuller. His eyes darkened as he remembered how one had fitted perfectly in the palm of his hand. Now they would overflow, the soft, silky, milk-pale flesh… He took a deep breath and pushed away the tactile image, but not before his body had hardened helplessly.

His sculpted lips twisted in a smile of self-mockery. For some reason around this woman his normal iron self-control took a holiday. What was it about her? It wasn't as if she were overtly sexual. She had a great body, as he knew only too well, but she didn't flaunt it. Look at the way she was dressed today, the shirt buttoned up to the neck, baggy creased trousers, and not a scrap of make-up. It was something elusive and intangible about her that, like smoke, defied his attempts to pin it down, control it.

As he scanned her tense features he wondered

why he looked at her and saw something different from everyone else... How many times at that damned wedding had he heard her referred to as serene?

She had not been serene that night they had spent together. He saw an image of her sitting astride him, her smooth thighs locked tight around his hips, her head thrown back and the sheen of sweat making her pale skin glisten in the darkness. She didn't look serene right now either; she looked like an exhausted young mother who had just received a nasty shock.

A beautiful but exhausted young mother. It would take more than lines of exhaustion bracketing her soft full mouth and dark shadows under her stunning blue eyes to diminish her looks.

He was in part at least responsible for putting the shadows there, he thought, and pushed away the stab of unaccustomed guilt. This was a situation that needed resolving. He had already missed out on the first precious months of his daughter's life and he was not going to miss out on the next while they bargained out a deal.

'Sorry, no cliff, but you could always impro-vise.' She liked to project the cool and calm image, but he had caught her off guard and peo-ple revealed more of themselves when they were off guard.

Izzy felt her anger drain away and with it her taste for this conversation. After all the heart rac-ing she felt horribly flat. 'You got me here, but what I don't understand is why you went to all this effort. Did you really expect me to stay? I'm taking Lily home, but don't think I won't send you the bill for this wasted journey, because I will!'

Even while she was hating him, at another level she was noticing the shadow of purple-black growth on his jaw and lean cheeks, the air of restless male vitality he exuded and how incred-ibly sexy he looked in the black jeans that clung to the long, muscular lines of his powerful thighs.

'Why not look around first? You might like what you see,' he drawled.

Izzy, refusing to acknowledge his reference to her drooling contemplation of his lean, muscle-packed body, met his knowing gaze with a defiant glare.

'Think of my home as your own.'

Home had a permanent sound and Roman had never actually had a home as such. He had over the years owned various properties because he liked the space and privacy and hotel suites gave little of either.

The only home he had known had been the town house near the university where his parents had worked and lived during term time, but his recollection of it was dim. Vacations had been spent on various digs in various far-flung corners of the globe, and when he was small he had been dragged along but usually left in the hotel room.

Then as he'd got older and bigger he had spent his summers either staying with friends' families or with a distant aunt of his father's in Tuscany.

'I thought you lived in Italy.'

'I do for a large part of the year, but recent developments make it necessary for me to have a British base, and I have never thought that the city is the best place to bring up a child.'

Izzy maintained her scepticism and filed away the statement to deal with later. Any spare energy she had was being used to stay upright. 'So you just popped out yesterday and bought this place?'

'Obviously not.'

A tiny gurgling sound quickly escaped Izzy's throat. The surprises just kept coming. *Roll with the punches, Izzy,* she told herself. *Tomorrow this will all be a memory.*

'I've owned it for…' he screwed up his eyes and glanced back at the building as he made the mental calculations '…two, almost three years now?'

Her sapphire eyes regarded him with disbelief. 'You're asking me?' How could a person own somewhere like this and not know how long they'd owned it for? If she had needed proof that Roman Petrelli lived in a different world than she did, she had it.

'Is it important? It's structurally sound and actually in better condition than I thought it would be.'

'I'm really not interested in your…' She stopped

and directed an incredulous look at his face. 'You make it sound like you've never seen it before.'

'I haven't.'

'You bought it without seeing it?' The idea seemed utterly preposterous to Izzy, who felt herself sinking back into a numb state of disbelief.

'It's what I do. It was a speculative purchase—the price was good.'

In other words, she thought scornfully, he had profited from the misfortunes of others.

'And I could afford to sit on it until the market—'

She cut across him, her voice flat as she asked, 'Why?'

'The place was bought at the height of the property boom by a—'

'I mean, why am I here?' Not that she would be for long. If it weren't for Lily being asleep, she would already have been trotting down that winding driveway, but if it weren't for Lily she wouldn't be here anyway.

She glanced towards her sleeping daughter cocooned in the baby carrier and experienced the familiar, almost suffocating swell of love, so intense that she felt light-headed. Although the light-headed feeling might have something to do with the fact that she hadn't been able to force down more than a couple of bites of the unappetising sandwiches she had bought on the train, and breakfast—God, that seemed like a lifetime ago—had been a slice of toast. She lifted a hand to her head and tried to remember if she had actually swallowed any of the toast.

'You look as if you're about to fall down.'

Izzy read the concern in his rough tone as criticism and her chin came up. She might look awful but it was damned rude of him to point it out.

And to add insult to injury he looked incredible, as always. He didn't seem capable of looking bad, no matter what the situation.

A deep visceral longing she refused to acknowledge twisted itself like a vine around her resentment as she made the journey from his booted feet to his glossy head… Somewhere around his taut middle her fingertips began to tingle.

By the time she reached his face other parts

tingled too, her cheeks were flagged with rosy heat and she was having a problem regulating her breathing. Long, lean and hard, he was more male than any man she had ever encountered.

She had always been dubious of the theory that in some throwback to a time of hunter-gatherers women chose an alpha male to father their children, but maybe…? Not that she had been looking for a father, just a lover, someone who could make her forget. Her blue eyes glazed as her thoughts drifted back.

And he had.

He had made her forget her name. She had taken pleasure from his body, revelling in a sensuality that she had not known she possessed. As the buried memories surfaced the past and present collided and for a moment she was looking at Roman and hearing, not the words coming from his lips, but a deep animal moan of pleasure that had been wrenched from his throat when she had curled her fingers around his silky, throbbing shaft…

CHAPTER SEVEN

'I SAID are you all right?'

Izzy blinked. This time there were no extenuating circumstances; this was simply unvarnished lust. She dodged Roman's gaze, denying the feelings, ignoring them in order to stay sane, stay safe.

'Fine.' Other than the ripples of hot sensation spreading outwards from a core that lay low in her belly. 'Will you stop looking at me like I'm some sort of specimen you want to dissect and pick apart?'

'If you'll stop undressing me with your eyes.'

Shame washed through her like icy water. Instead of remembering the sex between them, she should be remembering the awful hollow feeling she had felt the morning after. She was never,

ever going to feel like that again; she had learnt the hard way.

'I was not!'

He arched a brow and grinned. 'My mistake.'

Only it wasn't; he knew it and so did she.

'You wouldn't look so hot either if you'd just travelled on public transport with a small child. I suppose you think it's easy?' She slung him a belligerent glare just in case he thought she was canvassing the sympathy vote.

'I hadn't thought about it.' But he was now.

'You have no idea, do you?'

The mild contempt in her superior little smile would have irritated him had he not realised she was right. He glanced down at the sleeping child. Izzy was the one who had spent the sleepless nights with Lily, which made it doubly frustrating because she was resisting his attempts to make up for that now.

He put the carrier carefully down on the ground. 'Then tell me,' he suggested. 'I want to know.'

His focus had been totally on what he had missed out on, and not how different her life must be as a single mother from how it had been as a single girl. She had once been able to walk into a bar late at night and see someone she liked and now she could not just act on impulse. Maybe this was not such a bad thing. He had always considered himself pretty broad-minded and not a possessive man, but the idea of the mother of his child spending a night with a man, any man, filled him with a violent revulsion.

So far he had been preoccupied with resenting the time he had missed with his daughter and planning for the future; now for the first time he was realising how much her unplanned pregnancy must have changed her life too.

'I should have sent a car for you. Whoa, easy, let me...'

'What are you doing?' she snarled, backing away, dragging the handle of the folded buggy with her as the wheels gouged grooves in the thick gravel before it was removed from her grip.

'I thought you were going to faint.' He remained ready to step in because she had definitely swayed.

She narrowed her eyes. 'I don't faint.'

Roman controlled his growing irritation with her belligerent independence with difficulty. 'Fine, you don't faint,' he said, sounding bored. 'But wouldn't you be more comfortable continuing this conversation indoors, in the warm?'

'I'm not a child. You don't have to humour me.' Her eyes slid from his. She had no idea what it was about this man that brought out the very worst in her. She took a deep breath. 'All right.'

It was the practical response because she would not be comfortable continuing this conversation anywhere, but the wind had picked up while they were standing there and the chill would soon start to penetrate Lily's cosy padded jacket. She bent forward to pick up the baby carrier.

'Let me.' He paused, his hand above her own.

Izzy's fingers tightened over the carrier handle. After a brief internal struggle she stepped back, tucking her hands into her pockets. After all, it was only the carrier she was relinquishing to him. To make a fuss would only serve to highlight the insecurities she was struggling to hide. Roman's next comment suggested she wasn't doing this very well.

'I'm not trying to steal her, just helping.'

She knew he was looking at her but with her jaw set she stomped up the steps, her eyes trained on her feet. 'Steal her over my dead body.' She paused as she entered the hallway, unable to repress a startled admiring intake of breath.

'This place must have quite a history. Is the panelling original?'

'I wouldn't know.' His taste ran to the modern, and convenient. If they had been talking a private up-to-date gym, and the latest in computer technology, both items that this place lacked, Roman would have been interested.

'But just think about all the people who have lived here over the centuries.'

'I'm more interested in the plumbing, which is a bit basic. This way—the library is the second door on the left.' He nodded and stood to one side to let her go ahead of him.

Izzy, who would have liked to linger in this magnificent space, followed his directions and found herself in another equally pleasing room. It was being warmed by a fire burning in the massive stone grate and was lined with a row of south-facing mullioned windows that filled it with light.

'I thought nobody lived here,' she said, staring at the book-filled shelves.

'They came with the house.' His gaze moved over the book-lined walls. It was actually quite a pleasant room. 'Sit down, before you fall down.'

'I'm…' She responded to the pressure only because she couldn't stop her knees from trembling.

She sat there, her arms primly folded in her lap, and watched as he set the baby carrier down carefully and strolled across the room to the console table where a tray of coffee and sandwiches had been placed.

He pushed down the plunger of the cafetière, turning his head to enquire, 'Black or white?'

'White, no sugar.'

He piled a plate with some sandwiches and carried them across to where she was sitting, along with her coffee.

Her skin, dotted with freckles that stood out clear against the pallor, had an almost transparent quality. 'I don't want to get blamed if you pass out.'

'Are you going to stand over me while I drink this?'

'Yes.'

Pursing her lips she picked up the china cup. 'Anything for a quiet life.'

He laughed. 'Not so that you'd notice...and a sandwich,' he added when she put the cup back down.

Izzy slung him an irritated look, but she actually had three sandwiches, discovering she was starving. 'Satisfied?' she asked sarcastically as she pushed the plate away and sat back in her seat, folding one leg under herself. 'Do you have to stand there like some guard dog?'

She kept her expression neutral as his narrowed dark eyes moved over her face, but it was a struggle.

He didn't respond to her question, but his mouth did lift up at the corners as he flopped with lan-

guid grace into an armchair. Izzy felt the tension
in her shoulders lessen as he stretched his legs
out in front of him and crossed one ankle over
the other. It was easy to feel at a disadvantage
when he was towering over her.

She began to tap her toe on the polished wood
floor as he set his elbows on the aged leather
armrests.

'Some people would call this kidnapping.'

'A bit over the top, don't you think?' he drawled.

Her fury shifted up several notches as she
folded her arms across her heaving chest. She
sketched a smile and gave him a flat look.

'Oh, yes, I'm definitely overreacting.' The man
was unbelievable, as well as being totally unscru-
pulous and manipulative.

His dark brows lifted. 'The job is genuine. I offered it to you and you could have refused, but
you took it.' He rose in a graceful fluid motion
and angled a questioning look at her face. 'There
was no coercion involved.'

Izzy wished he would stay in one place or at
least keep sitting down; the man was like some

prowling jungle cat, all restless energy and un-predictability. In some ways she would have felt more relaxed with the animal he reminded her of in the room rather than the man himself!

'Genuine!' She almost choked over the descrip-tion. 'But I wouldn't have taken it if I'd known… known…'

'That you'd be living with me?'

The helpful insertion drew a gasp of horror from Izzy. 'Live with you?' she echoed.

Roman laughed.

'Or have you realised that this is too big a job for you?'

She struggled not to rise to the taunt and failed miserably. 'I'm up to the job.' It was her dream job and he knew it. She eyed him with seething dislike before squeezing her eyes closed as she made an attempt to regain some control of the situation and herself.

'This is a totally preposterous idea.' The tin-gling on her exposed nape made her open her eyes with a snap. Her radar had not misled her. He was close, too close, and crazily as she stared up into his deep-set, mesmerising eyes with those impossibly long lashes she wanted to step into his lean, hard body.

The effort not to made her shake, though she couldn't be sure that was the only thing making her shake. The fact was, physically he was like a narcotic to her and she had a terrible suspicion that, like any addict, one taste and she'd need a regular fix.

She dragged her gaze from his mouth, where it had drifted. *Don't taste, or look.*

'I hoped I'd be able to like you because you're Lily's father, but—'

'It is not necessary that you like your employer, and, speaking of Lily, it might be a good idea to keep your voice down if you don't want to wake her.' His sardonic mocking smile was briefly genuine as his glance touched the sleeping baby.

He was right, not that she'd admit it, but she did lower her voice as she snapped, 'I'm not working for you, end of story. And as for live with you, I'd prefer to live with a snake...' Izzy stopped. 'You're a cold, manipulative—'

'That's the façade. Deep down I'm soft and fluffy.'

She flung up her hands in a gesture of frustration and, fighting an urge to smile, sprang impetuously to her feet. She took a couple of steps towards the baby carrier before twisting back and facing him, her head thrown back, her eyes darkened to emotional navy as she glared at him.

'Do you take anything seriously?'

As if a switch had been flicked his sardonic smile was gone. He said nothing while he watched her chestnut hair bounce and settle silkily around her shoulders, then took a deliberate step towards her.

Her feet wanted to shadow the action, but she forced herself to step forward, not back, determined not to allow herself to show…fear? No, that was the wrong word. What was she feeling? What were the emotions swirling through her bloodstream? Excitement, loathing… She lifted a hand to her head, the contradictory mix making her feel light-headed. It would serve him right if she fainted. But in reality the idea of showing any weakness in front of him was terrifying.

Izzy shook her head, tuning out the distracting internal dialogue to think past the buzz in her head.

'I take being a father very seriously.'

His voice was low, almost soft, but the lack of emphasis only intensified the emotion behind the statement, causing Izzy to feel an irrational stab of guilt.

'And I will not be sidelined or fobbed off.'

'And I will not be pressured,' she threw back. 'This isn't about you and what you want. It's about what is best for Lily.'

'And that's you?'

'I'm her mother.'

'And that automatically makes you the best carer for her?' He elevated a dark brow and, shaking his head slowly from side to side, clicked his tongue in mock disapproval. 'Isn't that a rather sexist attitude, Isabel?'

'I'm not being sexist, I'm stating a fact—' She stopped abruptly mid-flow, the colour draining from her face so dramatically that he thought she was about to pass out. 'Are you suggesting…?' Her voice faded as jumbled images of lawyers and court hearings flashed through her head.

'Are you talking about contesting custody?' Legal battles did not come cheap and Roman had a lot of money. In theory she had faith in the legal system, but the thought of losing Lily made her feel hollow and more afraid than she ever had been in her life.

He opened his mouth to say he'd do whatever it took to have his daughter, then met with her stark blue gaze. Suddenly emotion kicked him hard in the chest; she looked so damned vulnerable. This situation combined with a chronic lack of sleep might have made his temper short, but Roman had never been a bully.

'No, I'm not.'

He had seen custody battles from a spectator's viewpoint and found them petty and distasteful. To use a child as a bargaining chip had always struck him as being abhorrent and in his new role as father he found the practice even more disagreeable.

'But I don't want my daughter raised to think a man's contribution to the bringing up of a child ends at the moment of insemination.'

Unable to shake the images of court battles, despite his denial, Izzy blinked up at him still feeling physically sick. 'Neither do I.' Her confusion was genuine.

He arched a satiric brow. 'Really? I'd assumed that you'd be carrying on the family tradition. You've got to hand it to your mother—she did at least practise what she preached.'

'If you want to know what I think, I suggest you ask me, not base your assumptions on the snatches of my mother's books you read.'

'Actually I read the entire book.' And having done so he had been amazed that her daughter was as relatively normal as she seemed. The woman had been a total zealot.

From his expression she was assuming Roman was not a fan. 'She wrote twenty.'

His lips tightened in a spasm of impatience.

'I think we both know which book I'm talking about. Did she actually believe all that drivel she wrote or did she just have a mortgage to pay off?'

Izzy took a deep breath and calmed her breathing. While she did not agree with a lot of what her mother had preached, she was not about to stand there while he sneered. 'My mother's book is considered a modern classic. She sparked debate, which can only be a good thing.' There was nothing her mother had liked more than a good argument.

'Do you make a habit of rubbishing people who are no longer here to defend themselves?'

The contempt in her voice made him flush, the colour running up dark under his golden-toned skin. 'So what did your mother teach you?'

She tilted her chin to a proud angle. 'My mother brought me up to make my own decisions.'

'Like having unprotected sex with a total stranger?'

He clenched his teeth, recognising the utter hypocrisy of his below-the-belt jibe the moment it left his lips. He still could not believe that he had been so criminally reckless; the only time in his life he had had unprotected sex had resulted in a child.

Izzy sucked in a breath. 'If you're trying to make me feel ashamed, don't waste your breath.' Her voice quivered and she bit her lip before husking, 'I already do.' She moved her head slowly from side to side in an attitude of bewilderment. 'I can't believe it was me that night.'

She had coped with the memory by treating it like some surreal, erotic, out-of-body experience. The wheel had fallen off that coping mechanism the moment Roman had appeared in her life. All the pent-up passion she had successfully denied had surfaced, no surreal dream any longer.

Roman's expression hardened. She was talking as if she'd been some awkward adolescent instead of a sensual woman who had known exactly what she wanted and had not been afraid to ask. 'Don't tell me,' he drawled. 'You didn't know what you were doing.'

She coloured angrily at his sarcasm. 'I'm not trying to deny responsibility.' In response to a faint whimper from the baby carrier she took hold of the handle and, on autopilot, began to rock it back and forth rhythmically. 'But I had just buried my mother, and I'd never actually done it before. What's your excuse, Roman?' Izzy froze and thought, 'God, did I say that out loud?'

'Yes.'

Izzy's eyes widened with shock before she pressed a hand to her mouth—a classic case of too little too late. In the stretching silence the sleeping child's regular breathing drew Roman's attention. He was still staring at his daughter when he finally spoke.

'Buried your mother?' His research had of course told him the woman was dead, he might even have read the date, but he had not made any connection.

Roman turned his head in time to see Izzy biting her lip. She met his eyes and tilted her head in acknowledgement. 'Cremated, actually.'

An image of her face that night floated into his head. He had been unable to take his eyes off her from the moment she had walked into the room, him and half the men in there. Amazingly she had seemed utterly oblivious to the lustful stares that had followed her.

He could still recall exactly what Isabel had been wearing when she'd walked into that bar. He could close his eyes and see the smooth oval of her face, her incredible skin, her startling sapphire eyes. So why hadn't he recognised something wasn't right?

When she'd kissed him, she'd been trying to forget. He should have seen it. Hadn't he been trying to achieve the same thing himself with the aid of a bottle and failing miserably?

'That day?'

She nodded.

Roman ground his teeth together and pressed the fingertips of one brown-fingered hand to the pulse spot throbbing in his temple before spearing both hands deep into his short sable hair.

She had used him!

And you didn't use her?

He closed his eyes and expelled a sharp sigh through clenched teeth. The truth was he *had* used her, sought to escape the total mess that was his life for a few stolen moments and find hot oblivion inside her. She'd been tight as a glove and they had shared a night of raw sex; her response had been uninhibited, elemental.

'How is it possible?' His dark brows flattened into an accusing line above his deep-set eyes. 'On such a day you should… Why were you alone? Someone should…' He stopped, a nerve in his lean cheek clenching.

'There wasn't anyone.' She seemed oblivious to how heart-rending that statement sounded as she related, 'That was the way she wanted it. She didn't want anyone, no sentiment, no ceremony, no service or wake.'

'And no closure for the loved ones left behind,' he rasped hoarsely. 'Though why am I surprised? Such a request is typical of a woman who never thought of anyone's needs but her own.'

The blighting condemnation of her dead parent drew a shocked gasp from Izzy. She let go of the handle and took a step towards him, her hands on her hips.

'Have you got a problem with strong women, Roman? Is that it?'

'You think your mother is a person to be admired?' Roman was bewildered by how protective Isabel was of the memory of someone who had lied to her all her life, deprived her of a father and, as far as he could see, been a friend, not a mother. 'You put your career on hold to spend time with your daughter. Did your mother ever put your needs above her own?'

'That wasn't a sacrifice,' she said quietly. 'I wanted to spend time with Lily. I didn't want to miss out on these early months. You have no idea how—'

'Precious they are? I think I have.'

Her eyes fell from his steady stare. 'She would probably have been equally happy and contented with a nanny.'

'I doubt that. You're a good mother.'

Izzy, conscious of a warm glow that shouldn't have been there—his approval meant nothing to her—took refuge in antagonism. 'And the point is I could do that, spend this time with Lily because the book you despised gave me financial independence. I appreciate you feel responsible,' she said stiffly. 'But I don't need your money and Lily and I are fine...'

'So what do you expect me to do? Walk away and say ring me? What happens when Lily gets ill or hates school? Do you really want to face those things alone?'

'If I need it the Fitzgeralds give me all the support I could want.'

'The Fitzgeralds? Do you think of yourself as one of them? Don't you feel an outsider?'

Alarmed by his perception, she lowered her gaze, allowing her dark lashes to screen her eyes from him.

'My independence means a lot to me and they respect that.' Which was more than he did. His constant prodding and prying were making her feel under siege and what was it about? All she'd been was a cheap one-night stand; the fact she'd had his child did not alter that.

'You must have been terrified when you found yourself pregnant and alone.' Roman struggled under the weight of unaccustomed guilt he felt when he thought of what she must have gone through. He saw her sitting there alone and afraid… His jaw clenched.

'I wasn't alone. Michael contacted me the same week I discovered I was pregnant.'

And what a week! In the space of two days she'd discovered that her wild night of passion with the handsome stranger had left her pregnant and received the letter from the man who was her father, inviting her to meet her new family.

'If I hadn't been pregnant…' She stopped as a sudden stab of emotion made her eyes fill. She blinked hard before adding with a hint of defiance, 'And, yes, feeling alone, I might not have agreed to meet him, but I did so my story had a happy ending.' She took out a tissue and blew her nose. The prosaic action touched Roman more than any tears would have.

'This story is not ended, Isabel. Our story is not ended.'

She shook her head, knowing he was right but still fighting it. Life had been simpler without him but here he was and he showed no signs of going away. For Lily's sake she knew she should make an effort, but they had nothing in common. He didn't even live in the same world as she did, but she could try at least not to be enemies.

'We don't have a story. It was just sex.' Staring at her clasped hands, she didn't see anger that flashed in his eyes. 'If I hadn't walked into that bar...' A shadow of confusion moved across her face like a cloud. 'I still don't know why I did that—I just saw the bar and...'

'Maybe it was fate?'

Her feathery brows lifted in surprise. He was the last person that she had expected to hear talk about fate. 'I don't believe in fate. I slept with an incredibly sexy man. That wasn't fate—it was hormones!' And given the opportunity she suspected nine out of ten unattached females would have done the same. She would have thought that she was the one who wouldn't have been attracted to him, but apparently she was no different. But he was, she thought as her glance drifted across the carved, perfectly symmetrical lines of his bronzed face, a dreaminess drifting into her expression. He made her think of some warrior with a poet's soul—his mouth was definitely poetry. The dreaminess was swallowed up by a stab of hungry longing as she studied the sensual outline.

'Incredibly sexy…?'

She jumped guiltily and dodged the wicked gleam in his eyes and found herself staring again at his mouth. Once she had started it was hard to stop. She cleared her throat and forced the words past the achy occlusion that made speaking difficult. It felt like wading through syrup.

'Like I'm not telling you anything you don't already know.'

He grinned but didn't deny it, she noticed. The wicked grin made him look years younger and even more wildly attractive.

'She must have been very young, your mother, when she died. It was unexpected?'

She nodded. Her mother had been a very young sixty-four.

'She was in her forties when she had me. She'd been ill for a while.' The onset of the illness that had struck her mother down had been insidious, although not immediately life-threatening. But she had been living with the effects of the degenerative disease that would eventually kill her. 'I was angry.'

'Yes.' He knew about anger.

During his stays on the oncology ward Roman had seen that reaction to death, seen enough people suffering the effects of shock and grief that it seemed to him that it was sometimes worse for the healthy ones who had to stand by helpless as their loved ones suffered and sometimes lost their battles for life.

The point was he should have seen the signs. He could recognise now with the wisdom of hindsight that she had been displaying all of them that night in the bar.

Roman closed his eyes and groaned.

Izzy looked at him uncertainly and he looked very pale when he looked at her again. A moment later he swore in his native tongue.

'You were in shock.' And he'd been too busy wallowing in self-pity to notice. He suddenly froze, his dark eyes swivelling her way. 'You just said you'd never done it before.'

Izzy expelled a choky sigh. Hell, just when she thought she was safe.

'Well, I don't make a habit of picking up strange men in bars. One-night stands are not really my style.'

He studied her down-bent head with a frown before moving his head slowly from side to side in a firm negative motion. 'No, that wasn't what you meant.'

Shifting uneasily under his severe gaze, she walked across to the sofa and sat down. 'I wish you wouldn't tell me what I mean. I am quite capable of saying what I mean.'

Roman refused to be distracted. 'And capable of lying, it would seem.'

'So you think one-night stands are my style...' She gave a little laugh. 'Thanks a lot.'

'It was your first time.' Even as he said it he rejected the statement; he had not actively avoided taking a virgin to bed, but then neither did he avoid meteorites. They both existed but the chances of encountering one were pretty remote.

She was not laughing or at the very least looking amused by such a preposterous notion. Instead she refused to meet his gaze and gave a defensive shrug.

CHAPTER EIGHT

'IT WAS a figure of speech.'

'A figure of speech as in you were a virgin.'

Roman's sarcasm made her flush and for a moment Izzy considered lying. But did it really matter if he knew the truth now? She thought not, so decided to come clean.

'My only time, actually.' She flashed him a warning glance and added fiercely, 'And don't ask me why because, to be honest, I don't know.'

She did have her suspicions, though, the most likely that being a twenty-year-old virgin had been a form of rebellion for her—not against parental control but against a total lack of parental control.

While other girls' parents gave them curfews and warned them of the dangers of teenage sex, her liberal mother had been telling her it was fine if she wanted to have boyfriends stay the night.

Izzy had always found such conversations excruciatingly embarrassing, but her mother had favoured what she called a frank and open exchange of views.

'You didn't act like a virgin.'

'How is a virgin meant to act, Roman?' She adopted an expression of fake interest as she started to feel angry. 'In the strange world you live in.'

'I live in the real world. You're the one who...' He stopped and pinned her with an intense, almost accusing stare. 'You must have had boyfriends?' he persisted, remembering how incredibly tight she'd been and her sharp gasp of shock as he had thrust deeply into her...

'For a semester I was in love with one of my mother's research assistants,' she recalled with a reminiscent grin. 'Happy now?'

He swallowed...happy? Happy that he had taken her innocence and not even noticed!

'So you had a relationship with this—?' A relationship that stopped short of sex. As he remembered her cool hands on his body and her hot, sweet tongue…that did not seem likely at all.

'Simon. No, it turned out he was gay.' She could smile now at the memory of her big moment when she had finally worked up the courage to ask him out. He had been nice about it and quite kind, but eventually the story had reached her mother, who had found it extremely amusing.

Unable to maintain contact with his intense stare, Izzy looked away.

Roman tried to think past the static buzz in his head. He felt numb. A virgin! It seemed impossible. The innate sensuality she projected had been one of the things that had drawn him to her. She was the most passionate creature he had ever held; the need to possess her had been all-consuming and she had matched his hunger and desire every step of the way.

'Why didn't you tell me?'

He still couldn't get his head around it, but it had to be true. There was no reason for her to lie. She had seemed totally at ease with her body, completely uninhibited and endlessly fascinated by his body. The question of her virginity had not even crossed his mind—why would it? She had seemed almost to know what he wanted before he had himself.

Face it, Roman, she was the best sex you ever had and she was a virgin. The staggering thought kept hitting him and the shock was not getting any less with each successive impact.

She turned her head, recognised the anger in his tense stance and shook her head. That was a reaction she had not anticipated. 'Why didn't you notice?' she countered.

At the time Izzy had presumed that he would.

She'd thought her sheer cluelessness would alert him and had desperately hoped it would not be a deal breaker.

But amazingly she hadn't felt awkward at all, or embarrassed or shy, which was insane because previously the idea of even being naked with a man had been something she didn't feel comfortable with. The entire intimacy thing had always been a problem for her, not because she was prudish but because she was choosy.

She had thought about it afterwards a lot and wondered if perhaps the fact that it had been anonymous sex, that he hadn't known her or had any preconceptions about her, had allowed her to let go. For once she didn't have to be the person everyone thought she was—nice, calm, sensible Izzy—she could be who she wanted to be. It had been the most liberating experience of her life.

Why hadn't he noticed? *Good question, Roman.* 'You were hardly shy.'

Did he expect her to apologise?

Her steady blue stare brought a dull flush of colour to his high cheekbones. 'Obviously if I'd known I'd have—' He stopped and thought, *Would I really have run a mile? Would I really have resisted the temptation to be her first lover?*

She'd given him a gift and he'd not noticed.

She acted as though it had been nothing and for some reason that made him angrier than anything else.

'I could have hurt you.'

'You didn't.'

'And you have never slept with any man since Lily was born?'

She gave a laugh. 'You really think that I've had the spare time or energy to have an affair? Besides it's a small place, everyone knows everyone and you can't sneeze without it being in the public domain.' That was one aspect of living in a small community that she hadn't come to terms with yet.

'So until you do have the time I'm the only man you've ever slept with.'

And Roman had never forgotten the night.

He ran a hand across his face and shook his head, unable to believe his total lack of control. He had never surrendered himself so totally to passion before or since that night; the searing fire of lust had totally devoured him. He had literally torn off his clothes like a fumbling boy who couldn't wait.

Izzy looked past him, trying not to see the image of his sculpted bronzed body in her head as she banded her arm around her midriff in an unconsciously protective gesture. It did not protect her from the memory of the warm silken feel of his skin against hers at the first shocking intimacy of his touch.

'There's no need to make such a big thing of it. We had sex,' she said, struggling to sound amused. 'That doesn't give us some magical bond.'

'Maybe not magic, but we have a bond—we have Lily.'

As if in response to her name the sleeping baby stirred, raising her voice in a fretful whimper. Izzy was up in a bound and beside the carrier.

'Per l'amor di Dio!' he rasped under his breath as he watched her bend forward, providing him with a perfect view of her pert round bottom.

Izzy, who was unfastening Lily, who was wriggling like an eel to escape, lifted her head at the sound of his soft curse and, misinterpreting its cause, cautioned, 'Babies don't time their demands to suit you, Roman.'

The man needed a reality check. Maybe he would be less eager to be involved with Lily when he realised the demands that went with a small baby. 'For the first three months I was rarely dressed before midday.'

From where he was standing that did not seem a bad thing to Roman.

She shook her head to toss back a strand of hair that was tickling her nose as she lifted up Lily. 'I can't remember the last time I visited the hairdresser's.' When she got back home, Izzy decided, she would take up Michelle's suggestion they let Grandad babysit while they went for a spa day treat.

'You have beautiful hair.' He remembered it soft and lustrous spread out on the pillow as she had reached up for him and pulled him down.

Her eyes flew to his face where the raw hunger stamped on his bronzed features made her heart thud. It was Lily's small foot landing a lucky and painful kick in her stomach that broke the sexual thrall that had rapidly sucked her into its sensual vortex.

Her laughter was tinged with a good dollop of breathless relief as she kissed the sole of the bare foot that had pulled her away from the brink of making a total fool of herself.

'Now, what have you done with that sock… eaten it?'

'It's there.' Roman bent to pick up the lost item.

'Thank you.' She held her hand palm up rather than risk touching his long brown fingers. He probably knew but by this point Izzy was past caring. 'She's always losing socks,' she said, tucking it in the pocket of her cardigan. As if picking up on the tension in the air, Lily began to squall irritably.

Roman regarded her red face with a concerned frown. 'Is she ill?'

'No, she's hungry.'

'How do you know?'

'It's generally a matter of elimination. Is there somewhere I could heat up her food? Where did I put the bag?' She looked around for the holdall.

'I've got it.' Roman's brows shot up as he picked up the bag with the pink handle and cheerful teddy-bear characters. '*Dio*, what have you got in here?'

Izzy gave a rundown. 'Food, drink, nappies, a change of clothes and some toys.' She reeled off the items that she rarely travelled anywhere without. 'Somewhere I can heat up...?'

'Yes, of course, I'll show you.' He held open the door for her to pass through in front of him. 'The kitchen is this way, I think.' He led the way through a door into a stone-flagged inner hall. 'And there are rooms prepared upstairs if you want to change her.'

Before Izzy could protest he added, 'It's too late now to make the journey back to Cumbria. I can't promise luxury but the place is perfectly habitable, just a little tired décor wise. I'm not sure if you'll want to do any structural remodelling but—'

Trotting a little to keep up with his long stride, Izzy stared up at him. 'Why do you persist in acting as though it's a done deal? Don't you understand the meaning of no?'

He pushed open a heavy door and nodded for her to go through before him. 'Depends on the context. So what do you think? Could you do something with it?'

She might hate cooking.

She might be a domestic goddess.

It seemed impossible that they could know so little about one another and yet they had made a child.

He stood back and watched her look around the room.

'A bit small?' he suggested. 'The original kitchen is on the lower ground floor used for storage now. It could be reinstated. I'd thought possibly knocking through, incorporating the smaller rooms and knocking out the wall replacing it with glass and putting in a south-facing terrace...?'

The ambitious suggestion drew a laugh from Izzy.

'This house has got to be listed?'

He nodded.

'Listed means you can't just knock down walls. Besides, this is a lovely room. Not that it's any of my business,' she tacked on quickly. 'Will you stop looking so smug? I'm not staying. And if you want to make yourself useful, watch Lily while I organise her food.' She placed the baby on the floor and held out her hand for the bag.

Roman took a wooden tractor from the top of the bag, then handed it to her. 'Are you always so bossy?'

'Does that mean the wedding's off?'

The tentative rapport immediately vanished in a big black hole of heavy tension.

'This isn't about scoring points.' His expression remained stern as he bent down and pushed the wooden toy across the ground to the baby, who immediately grabbed it and pushed it in her mouth.

'Is that safe?'

Izzy, still stinging from his reproach, glanced over. 'Fine. She's teething—everything goes in her mouth.'

Roman straightened up, leaned back against a counter and stood watching while Izzy moved around the room until, in the act of pulling a lid off a jar, she was unable to bear his silent scrutiny another second. She stopped and expelled a sigh through clenched teeth.

Straightening her slender shoulders, she put down the jar and turned to face him. 'So, all right, it's not a joke or about scoring points. What is it about?'

Her eyes were incredible, the deepest, purest blue he had ever seen.

She arched a delicate brow. 'Well?'

'This is about damage limitation.' And controlling his desire to touch her. He cleared his throat. 'It's about you admitting you can't do it all yourself. It's about me being allowed to take my share of the responsibilities. You don't like this house? Fine. I…we can find something you do like.'

'I like where I live.' He just kept missing the point.

'That cottage, there's not enough room to swing a cat there.'

'My cottage!' she exclaimed. 'You have never seen my cottage. You don't even know where I live!'

'I may not have had an invite but be real, Isabel. Of course I know where you live, and I'm assuming your house is not dissimilar in size to your neighbour's, who kindly did ask me in after I admired her dahlias.'

'You…you…how dare you? You wouldn't know a dahlia from a daisy.'

'Now there you go again, making snap judgements based on what?'

'I don't care if you have green fingers.' Actually his fingers were brown and long and sensitive. Hand pressed to her fluttering stomach, Izzy dragged her gaze upwards and finished angrily, 'I won't tolerate being spied on and manipulated.'

His languid air vanished. 'And I will not tolerate my child living in a house paid for by Michael Fitzgerald.' Michael Fitzgerald was the least of Roman's concerns. There was no man in Isabel's life right now, but how long would that situation continue? How long before some man wanted to move in and bring up his daughter?

Izzy was taken aback by the underlying venom in his tone. 'What have you got against Michael?'

'Nothing. I barely know the man,' Roman cut

back, looking impatient. 'Other than the fact he has an excellent reputation as a horse breeder.'

'For the record, I rent the cottage, not Michael. He offered to help financially, but I refused.' She lifted her chin. 'I can pay my own way.' She bent and scooped up the baby.

'Did Michael ask who the father was?' If the roles had been reversed he would have tracked down the man responsible and… But he was the reckless bastard responsible and it was his job to protect his own daughter.

Izzy shook her head. 'No.' She suspected that Michelle had a lot to do with this restraint.

'But he knows now.'

'Obviously Michelle told him.'

Izzy brought her lashes down in a protective sweep. Michael's response, she realised in retrospect, had initiated their first father and daughter dispute. She had found herself placed in the strange position of defending Roman.

He had eventually cooled down and had even apologised after Michelle had supplied a large dose of common sense, but the subject was still a sensitive one.

'But don't worry, it doesn't have to go any farther. They won't tell anyone else.' She gave a sudden laugh, her glance moving from Lily to Roman. 'They won't have to if anyone sees you together.'

'People are going to know, Isabel.'

She swallowed. 'I suppose so.'

He studied her face and felt his anger grow without knowing why. 'You look delighted by the prospect.'

'Are you telling me you are? That you don't care about people talking and speculating?' She curled up inside at the idea of being the butt of gossip again.

'I do not care about what people say about me.'

Exasperated, she rolled her eyes. 'I get the message, but could you lower it a bit? The testosterone levels are giving me a headache…and before you come over all huffy,' she said wagging her finger at him, 'remember you don't care what people think about you.'

His taut expression faded to one of reluctant amused admiration. 'Huffy? Is that even a word?'

'And here was me thinking your English was better than mine.'

'And I said think not say, smart little witch.'

'Oh, I'm sure people only say what you want to hear,' she observed, thinking that it would take a brave person to cross swords verbally or otherwise with this man.

'Not all people. Tell me, if our paths had not crossed what did you plan to tell Lily when she asked about her father?'

Izzy's narrow shoulders lifted. 'Truthfully I don't know.' Her eyes drifted to his mouth.

'You're blushing!' he accused suddenly.

Izzy wasn't about to tell him that her own thoughts were making her blush—thoughts about his mouth.

'It's warm in here.'

'You think?' he drawled, wondering why she was lying.

Izzy ignored the scepticism in his smile. 'I don't want to lie to her.'

He arched a brow. 'But you would.'

'Truth?' She gave a helpless shrug and paused, seemingly lost in her own thoughts until he prompted.

'Truth?'

Her blue eyes connected with his. 'I don't know. I mean, at what age do you say to your child, I don't actually know your father's name—he was a one-night stand who picked me up in a bar?'

'Actually, if we're being totally accurate, you picked me up.'

She flashed him an insincere smile. 'Well, thanks for that.'

He tipped his head. 'Any time.'

'But a child wants to feel they were conceived with...' She stopped and lowered her gaze, unable to say love and invite his cynical retort. 'Well, that they at least knew each other's name and it wasn't some quickie...'

The coarse description brought a flash of anger to his eyes. 'The point is that parents do not discuss their conception with the children, unless your mother was the exception. Did she feel the need to share the gory details?'

'She told me my dad was a test tube.'

This casual revelation caused his winged ebony brows to hit his hairline. 'What?'

Izzy, who was wiping a stray blob of banana from her daughter's curls, turned to face him. She held the box of wet wipes in one hand, the used wipe in the other hand as she tried to sweep the stray strands of hair from her face with her forearm. One stubborn culprit remained, tickling her nose.

'Let me.'

His eyes were dark and intense as he looked down into her upturned features. Izzy stood very still, not even breathing as he took the silky hank of hair in his long brown fingers, brushing her cheek and jaw as he tucked it carefully behind her ear.

He took for ever and every second was torture. Her insides were quivering, her outsides were burning and her skin was so sensitive that every light touch of his fingers felt like a burning brand.

Torture was not an exaggeration for the effort it took for her not to react to either the impulse to slap his hand away or the contrasting and equally strong impulse to grab it and rub her cheek into his palm.

She started breathing again as he retook his place propping up the counter. Tall, elegant and not even slightly affected, but why would he be? Only crazed women got turned on by someone tidying them up. *If he'd wiped the banana out of my hair I'd probably moan and scream, 'Take me!'* she thought with a grimace of self-disgust.

Dropping the soiled wipe in a waste bin, Izzy grunted a thanks and picked up the threads of her narrative.

'She told me my dad…well, that I didn't have one. I always believed that I was the product of artificial insemination.'

'Madre di Dios!' he exclaimed.

'It seemed normal to me.' Until she had mentioned it to her friends in school.

'So when did she tell you the truth?'

'She didn't. She left a letter for me to read after she died. She left one for Michael too.'

'And you had read that letter on the day we...' He inhaled and closed his eyes, breathing through clenched teeth. 'Of course you did.' He bit out a savage-sounding curse that drew Izzy's attention to his face.

His mouth was taut and his narrowed eyes were almost black. 'Are you mad with me?' she asked, her voice rising to an indignant squeak. 'Because I don't see why.'

'No, I am not mad with you.' He framed the words from between clenched teeth. 'I am mad with me.' He took a deep breath, making a visible effort to put a lid on his emotions before continuing, his voice a careful monotone as he delivered his opinion.

'I think that how Lily was conceived is irrelevant. It is how she is brought up that is important. Do you agree?'

She nodded warily. Where was he going with this? 'Of course.' What else could she say?

'She deserves to be brought up to know she is wanted, cared for emotionally and physically.'

When you said it that way it sounded so simple, but it wasn't and he knew it. Roman sketched a small self-mocking smile. An ultra-confident person, he had never been plagued with self-doubt, he thrived on challenges, but this fatherhood thing scared him.

'I don't know what kind of father I'll be,' he admitted.

Would he be a good father...? He found the idea of being responsible for another person incredibly daunting.

'But I know I won't neglect her or leave her alone. I won't let her get on the wrong train when she is ten and have to find her way from Brighton in the dark to—' He stopped abruptly, adding in a hard voice, 'The point is, the things parents do impact on a child... I don't want my child to pay the price for my mistakes.'

'Roman, were you that little boy?'

CHAPTER NINE

'MY PARENTS were in love.' Roman would not personally call their obsessive, symbiotic relationship love or even healthy, but his was not the generally held opinion. 'Their love did not stretch to a child. So, yes, I was that child.'

Izzy didn't know what to say. 'I'm sorry.'

She could tell from his body language that he was regretting giving even this meagre amount of personal information.

'I am going to be part of Lily's life and you can deal with it like an adult or...'

'Or?'

'I'm not the bad guy, Isabel. Don't make me one,' he said quietly. 'Look, maybe I shouldn't have tricked you into coming here, but you wouldn't talk to me, and the marriage thing—I scared you. I get that, but sometimes I say things without thinking them through.'

'You were rushing me, pushing. You wouldn't give me time to think.'

He dragged a hand through his hair and levered himself away from the counter. 'I'm not good at waiting.'

'You mean you're impatient?'

An expression she struggled to read flickered in his deep-set eyes before he shrugged his shoulders.

'I like to live in the here and now, not waiting for some tomorrow that might...' He stopped, leaving the sentence unfinished.

She understood the significance of that look now.

'But there is for you?' she said, suddenly needing reassurance on this point. Well, he was Lily's father. 'A tomorrow, you mean...a lot of tomorrows?' He looked the picture of lusty health but who knew?

At the time he had not discussed his illness with her because from his experience the moment anyone heard the word cancer they saw *it* and not him. It remained a subject that he avoided.

'Who knows? But I have every intention of being around to see Lily grow up.'

The knot of anxiety in her stomach relaxed as she released a tiny sigh of relief.

He stepped away from the door he'd opened and Izzy saw the interior of a pantry that was filled with baby equipment. 'I asked Gennaro to pick up a few things,' he said, pulling out a wooden high chair and setting it beside the large wooden table that was set in the centre of the room. 'Is this any good?'

'A few things!' she exclaimed, staring at the stacked shelves and noticing that the piles of nappies were in every size available. 'It looks like he bought the shop. Yes, that's great,' she admitted, depositing Lily in the chair.

She fastened the bib around Lily's neck and took the spoon from the bowl of baby food, handing it to Roman.

'You got to start somewhere.' *Please do not*

make me regret this. 'It's just a spoon, so don't start with the smug smile,' she warned.

Roman saw the blue plastic spoon for what it was: an olive branch and the first thawing in her attitude. Careful to keep his expression clear of the smugness she accused him of, he took it.

Fifteen minutes later the tension in the atmosphere had diminished considerably and the food in the bowl seemed to be evenly distributed between the baby, Roman and the floor.

'That is not as easy as it looks. Did she actually swallow any?'

'Enough,' Izzy murmured, taking the empty bowl and spoon and dropping them in the deep old-fashioned stone sink. She looked at him surreptitiously through her lashes as he rolled down his sleeves. Would any of his boardroom colleagues have recognised their elegant designer-suit-wearing boss?

She hardly recognised him herself.

Could she talk to this man without feeling overpowered?

Perhaps she should try?

'You do know that I was always perfectly willing to give you access to Lily… It never even entered my head not to, but when a man you don't know proposes…'

'I did not propose. *Dio*, if I had gone down on one knee and said you made me complete I could understand your reaction.'

The mockery in his tone stung. 'Maybe I want the one-knee approach…' She saw his expression and added hastily, 'But not from you, obviously.'

His ebony brows hit his hairline. 'Now that I didn't see coming… You're a romantic.'

He made it sound as if she had some embarrassing disease. 'I don't have a romantic bone in my body.'

'Good, then let's discuss this like two rational people.'

Presumably rational and romantic were two things that did not coexist in his eyes.

'I'm listening.'

'You said to me that this is not about me or how I feel, but about Lily, and you are right, but are you not willing to concede that Lily would be better off with two parents?'

'She has two parents. They don't have to have the same address. I am willing to discuss a plan so long as you don't stray into la-la land again. We have Lily in common and nothing else...'

If she did ever consider marriage he was everything the man she married wouldn't be. She knew that there were women who found controlling behaviour a turn-on, but she had never wanted to be dominated by a man and Roman Petrelli was the ultimate in male chauvinism.

'We have lust...a chemical reaction in common.'

She was unprepared for the comment and the breath left Izzy's lungs in one sibilant gasp, but before she could contest the statement, before she could stop the hot, lurid images playing in her head, he added drily, 'And there is a lot of historic precedent for basing marriage on just that, though the days when the only way a nice girl could get any was with a ring on her finger are long gone.'

'Lust?' The scorn she tried to inject into her voice just didn't come off.

He lifted a sardonic brow and laughed. 'Come off it, *cara*. You're not suggesting that you don't want to rip my clothes off...' His heavy-lidded gaze slid down her body before he added, 'I can feel the heat coming off you from here.'

His husky rasp stroked her nerve endings into painful tingling life. 'You carry on thinking that if it makes you happy,' she recommended. 'But it doesn't matter what situation you manufacture where we can play happy families, I'm not playing along.'

'Tell me who had the best upbringing—your siblings or you?'

The comparison was unfair and he had to know it. 'I wasn't a deprived child. Ruth was a good friend. Look, marriage isn't for me but I accept that for some people who are in love... I suppose you don't believe in love?' she charged, annoyed by the sneer curving his lips as he listened.

'Oh, but I do. My own parents were as deeply

in love from the moment they met until the day they died.'

'You make that sound like a bad thing,' she accused. 'I know you didn't have a happy childhood,' she said, recalling his earlier comments.

'I think that love, the all-consuming variety, can be selfish and destructive, but more relevantly does not make the people in love good people or, for that matter, good parents.'

Izzy fought off a stab of sympathy. 'Didn't you get on with your parents?' Her mother might not have been the warm, fluffy, hands-on type of parent, but Izzy had always known she was loved and valued.

'I barely knew them.'

It was his offhand tone as much as the statement that made Izzy blink in confusion before comprehension struck. For a moment empathy dampened her antagonism.

'Oh, I thought...' She half lifted her hand to clasp his arm, the physical gesture instinctive, but thought better of it, instead threading her thumbs in the belt loops of her jeans. 'I'm sorry. I didn't know they died when you were young.'

'My parents died six years ago when I was twenty-five, but I was always on the periphery of their lives.' It had seemed appropriate that they had died together when the cruise ship they were on struck a smaller vessel. The damage to the ship had been minor but in the subsequent confusion and hysteria several people had gone overboard, including his parents.

'The reason couples like your father and Michelle have a successful marriage is because they are both intelligent people who work at it. They create a stable environment in which to bring up their children.'

'They're in love.'

'In love?' His scorn was overt. 'What does that mean exactly? People fall in and out of love every day of the week. How many times have you seen some celebrity being interviewed waxing lyrical about their soul mate?'

'Is the sneer for celebrities or love?'

Nostrils flared in distaste, he spoke over her

sarcastic interruption. 'The next week their acrimonious break-up is being reported everywhere.'

'We're not celebrities.' Although, she mused, her glance drifting from the strong symmetry of his bronzed features to his body, there were a lot of Hollywood stars who worked hard to get what Roman had and never reached that elevated level of jaw-dropping, sexy perfection. It was hard to believe that she had…

'But we are parents.'

Izzy started, her guilty eyes flying back to his face. 'I know that,' she gritted out. 'What I don't know is why you have this weird fixation with getting married. It's not rational.'

'And the idea that you fall in love with someone at twenty and still love them thirty years later is? Being in love does not make a good marriage or good parents.'

'So what are you saying exactly?'

'I'm saying that we can be married and be good parents, and not be in love. No!' he said, lifting a hand to still the protest that trembled on her tongue. 'I know your instinct is to shoot down my arguments in flames, but think for one moment. We have a child—'

'You keep saying that like it might have slipped my mind!'

'Do we not owe it to her to explore all possibilities? I am not suggesting we rush up the aisle— living in close proximity might reveal that we are totally incompatible—but I am suggesting living here for a period of time, long enough for me to get to know my daughter and for us to see how such an arrangement would work.'

'You're suggesting a trial...what...?' She couldn't bring herself to ask if he was expecting her to sleep with him.

He gave a smile as though he could read her mind. 'There are many rooms in this house. We can be as close or as far apart as we wish.'

'It's a mad idea.'

'And you can flex your creative muscles, tackle a room at a time, make it as you would wish it if you lived here. Money no object.'

'Is that the carrot?'

'For some women the chance to spend some

quality time with me would be the carrot, which brings us back to lust. That night we spent together still feels very much unfinished business to me.'

'No, it's totally finished for me…completely!' She illustrated how completely with a sharp sweeping motion of her hand.

He greeted her hot denial with a look of polite disbelief, which set Izzy's teeth on edge.

'As you wish. If you agree to give this a go, I will agree not to propose to you again until we have established we can live together without wanting to kill one another. For the record there is a dower house on the estate that, if the worst comes to the worst, I can sleep in. Such an arrangement, though not ideal, would be acceptable to me in the future. I know someone who has bought the house next door to his ex-wife so that he can see his children every day.'

'You would live in the dower house here?' She was startled by the offer.

'We can live wherever you choose.'

She was impressed; how could she not be? He

was prepared to totally turn his life upside down, relocate—anything, it seemed, for his daughter. Considering this, what he was suggesting no longer seemed such a big ask.

'All right, I'll give it a go.'

Roman greeted her choice with a nod of his head, but inside he was punching the air in triumph.

CHAPTER TEN

IZZY spent a couple of hours exploring the warren of rooms. She had felt fewer qualms about leaving Lily with Roman than she had imagined she would. It was hard to walk around the historic building and not be excited by the, what had he called it…*potential*?

She smiled to herself. The place had that, all right.

The room that had been made up for her was pretty and south-facing. There was a brand-new cot and stacks of fresh linen in the adjoining dressing room and beyond that a bathroom. Opening another door, she found herself in a room that was a twin to her own. The folded clothes on the bed said that she was standing in Roman's room.

Cosy, she thought. *Umpteen rooms and he's next door?* Was she appalled by this obvious manoeuvring? No, she was excited. The discovery shook her a lot more than seeing his boxer shorts neatly stacked!

She had anticipated sharing some sort of romantic dinner with him so she was a bit thrown when even before she had put Lily to bed he explained that there were urgent things he needed to attend to in the library, which it seemed was to be his temporary office.

Having decided to repulse any advances he made, she was miffed not to be afforded the opportunity! If this was part of a 'treat 'em mean keep 'em keen' strategy, it was working, because as she sat enjoying a lonely microwave supper she thought of little but him.

She fell to sleep listening for the creak of floorboards and woke some time later, her maternal sensors picking up Lily's cry.

'Darling, it's all right, Mummy's here.'

She stopped on the threshold. She wasn't the only one who was here. Roman was standing over the cot, winding up the mobile suspended over it. He turned and mimed a hushing gesture.

Lily's heavy eyelids were already closing; her lashes lay blue black against her rosy cheeks.

Izzy nodded, aware rather belatedly that she was wearing only her nightdress. She smiled and tiptoed her way back into her own room, her heart beating faster because she knew he was following her.

She turned just as he was closing the adjoining door carefully behind him.

He struggled to keep his eyes on her face. 'I'm glad I saw you.' The semi-sheer ankle-length nightdress she wore was rendered virtually transparent by the lamplight, revealing the curvaceous outline of her body and the strategic dark areas… 'I meant to catch you before you went up. I'm sorry I had to leave you on your first night, but there were some contracts I had to sort. I don't mean to bore you. Did you find everything all right?'

'Yes, thank you…fine.' He looked like the living incarnation of everything that was male and raw and powerful. He was the very opposite of her and things inside her shifted and tightened as she stared at him.

He tipped his head, feeling the flare of attraction between them so strongly that it made his blood burn. This was only ever going to work if he let her dictate the pace, one false move on his part and... 'Right, then, I'll... Sleep well.'

'No.'

He turned back, a question in his eyes.

She stood there wanting him so much it hurt; every cell ached with the wanting. She wanted to feel his body hard and male, smell his skin and enjoy the tactile sensations of flesh on flesh. She wanted to tangle her fingers in his hair, taste... oh, taste...!

How long could she carry on resisting and why should she?

The escalating desires were consuming her, sapping her ability to think beyond these basic primal needs. She felt as if she were drawn towards him by some invisible cord that was reeling her in. She'd been fighting so hard, fighting not to admit how much she wanted him, and why not…? The time to be cautious had been two years ago; this was no leap in the dark.

Why not?

Uneasily aware that her defiance masked a desperate need that she didn't want to think about, she faltered. 'I…I don't want you to go…'

The broken plea had barely left her lips and he was at her side, framing her face in his big hands, kissing her.

He felt his control slipping away as her hand slid up his back and she whispered in his ear, 'I want to feel your skin.'

He pulled back only far enough to rip off his shirt and place her hands on his bare chest.

Eyes slumberous and passion-glazed, Izzy ran her hands over the planes and ridges of muscle on his torso and up over his broad shoulders. Need ached through her, sweet like honey, sharp like a knife. 'Your skin feels like silk.'

She ran her tongue across her lips and the action caused his eyes to darken. He pulled her into him, causing their bodies to collide. His open mouth covered hers, hot and moist, his firm lips moving with the same erotic, sensuous motion that his hips were against her lower body.

'Yes…oh, God,' she murmured against his mouth. She was spinning out of control and she loved it!

Still kissing her, he scooped her up in his arms and carried her across the room. When they reached the bed he placed her on her feet.

The febrile glow in his eyes made her dizzy as he caught hold of the bottom of her nightdress. She lifted her arms to help him and a moment later her nightdress hit the opposite wall.

He lifted her bodily onto the bed, kneeling over her prone form, and allowed his burning gaze to roam freely over her naked body.

Izzy experienced a moment's doubt; the last time he had seen her she had not had a child— her body had changed since then. Her hips were wider, her breasts fuller and softer; she had a woman's body now.

Would he like what he was seeing?

'You are so beautiful…more beautiful.' He had

never wanted a woman like this in his life; it was the same as that night, only more so.

Izzy released the breath she had been holding and reached up and dragged him down, her hands deep in his dark hair as she pulled his mouth to her aching breasts. He took first one hardened nipple in his mouth and then the other, drawing a series of moans and gasps from Izzy as she writhed beneath him in a frenzy of desire.

She bit into his shoulder, sliding her arms around his back and arching as she tangled her fingers deeper into his hair, bringing his mouth to hers. She sank her tongue between his lips, wanting to taste him, wanting him to taste her.

She was gasping for breath and almost delirious with pleasure when he began to kiss a path down her throat. Her body was limp and pliant as he pulled her onto her side, looping one of her thighs across his hip as he kneaded her buttock, his fingers sinking into the soft springy flesh. He eased a finger along the damp cleft between her legs, drawing a low moan from her parted lips as he stroked her slowly and rhythmically.

He rolled her onto her back and she lay there looking at him with big passion-glazed eyes as he tore off his remaining clothes and returned to her.

'Don't close your eyes,' he insisted. 'I want you to watch.'

She did watch as his hands were on her body, touching her everywhere, lighting fires and massive conflagrations until she burned all over and deep inside, releasing all the loneliness and fear that had been hiding there.

Izzy was dimly aware of a voice that sounded as if it was coming from a long way off, a voice begging and pleading, realising with a sense of shock that it was hers when he whispered in her ear.

'I can't wait either, *cara*.'

She arched her body, lifting off the bed as he slid into her in one hard thrust. She clung to him, her face pressed into his shoulder, her arms wrapped around his sweat-slicked muscled back as he filled her again and again until she almost fainted with the sheer bliss of it.

She climbed so high it felt as if she were flying. Then as the vibrations that began deep inside her grew, she fell, losing a sense of self as her entire body shook in a series of shattering sensory explosions.

Later, when their sweat-slick bodies had cooled, he pulled her face from his shoulder and ran a finger down the thin pink line low on her abdomen.

'Tell me about that.'

'I had a long labour and things went wrong... I had a Caesarean.'

She saw his expression and touched his face with her hand. 'It was nothing major... I just wish I could have seen her when she was born.'

She had given birth alone and in pain and she was the one offering comfort.

'Now we both have our scars,' she teased, reaching down to touch those on his leg. 'They're from your illness...?' She had thought when she first saw them that they were from an accident.

'I had bone cancer. I was lucky it was picked up early when they X-rayed me after a climbing fall. Not pretty.'

'They're part of you,' she said, looking surprised.

'Lauren didn't think so. I don't blame her—any woman would have felt the same.'

Izzy raised herself up on one elbow, wondering if he defended the indefensible because he still loved her. 'You have a very low opinion of women.'

Roman looked at her fondly. 'Not everyone has your strong stomach.'

Not everyone had a man like Roman in their bed, including the shallow and stupid-sounding Lauren.

As Gennaro pulled into the outside lane of the motorway Roman closed his laptop.

'Are things all right?' Last night had been the first time he had spent a night away from Izzy and Lily. He had spent most of the time wondering what they were doing. He wouldn't have gone at all if Izzy hadn't insisted.

Parenting was a steep learning curve. The time he spent working he felt guilty he was neglecting his family and the time he spent with his family he felt guilty he was neglecting work.

When he had discussed it with Izzy she had laughed and said, 'Welcome to my world, big boy. Women have been feeling that way for ever and a day!'

Izzy... The situation was working out better than he could have hoped. There was just one development that he had not expected. People said things in the throes of passion they did not necessarily mean, but three times now she had moaned, *'I love you!'* Roman was certain that she was just babbling nonsense; she had to be. The whole point of their relationship was to be together without falling in love...

'What's that?' Izzy asked, looking at the gift-wrapped box.

'Open it and see.'

She flashed him a smile and unpicked the prettily tied bows, resisting the impulse to tear them. She carefully unfolded the beautiful layers of tissue paper to reveal the item that lay beneath.

'It's beautiful!'

'How do you know? It's still in the box! It's a dress.' He had given women gifts on many occasions, many more expensive than this one, but he had never watched his gifts being opened before. Now he found himself feeling almost nervous, experiencing a desire for them to be pleased.

Taking hold of the fabric, she took it out, gasping as the beaded silk unfolded to reveal the most glamorous dress she had ever seen.

'It's beautiful.' Her wide eyes took in details of the low-waisted, heavily beaded, twenties-inspired dress. It was made of silver-grey silk; the tiny beads arranged in geometric patterns were silver and they winked and caught the light. 'Real golden age Hollywood,' she enthused.

'It is only a dress.'

It was nothing.

Conscious that through his sophisticated eyes her reaction might seem a little over the top, Izzy damped down the enthusiasm levels of her response as she pointed out sensibly, 'But I'll never wear it.' Holding the dress against her, she studied her reflection in the antique mirror she had recently installed on the opposite wall.

'Why not?' he asked. She reminded him of a child opening her presents on Christmas morning.

She arched a delicate brow. 'When did you last see me in anything that didn't involve jeans?'

She looked very good in jeans, he thought as his eyes slid to her tightly rounded derrière. Especially the pair she was wearing now, which clung in all the right places.

'You will have an opportunity tonight.'

'Tonight?'

'You have spent the last three weeks in some sort of self-imposed exile.' As exiles went the one they had shared had not been a trial, but enough was enough. 'We are going out.'

'Is this you asking?'

'No, this is me being masterful, or, if you prefer, autocratic?' He grinned and she thought just how charming he was.

'It is all arranged. I have asked Chloe to baby-sit. You have no problem with that?'

Chloe was an art student who had been helping Izzy out with the sample boards.

'It seems to me that she is level-headed and responsible.'

'Yes, she is.' And Lily loved her.

'So tonight we will dress up and dine together.'

'But why? Do you want to check out my table manners or something?' she teased. 'Check out I'm not a social liability before you sign on the dotted line,' she added, only half joking now.

Wishing she had not introduced a reference to the subject that was always the elephant in the room, Izzy veiled her eyes, but not before her cheeks had grown self-consciously pink.

'I have had no opportunity to show you off and it is your birthday, isn't it?'

Her blue eyes widened as they flew to his face. 'How did you know?'

He thought of the report he had downloaded on his laptop. He did not imagine that its existence would endear him to her, so instead he turned the question back on her. 'I think the question should be why didn't you tell me?'

Izzy was conscious of a fizz of excitement. The idea of dressing up and eating a meal with an incredibly handsome man was not totally awful. If you had fallen deeply, hopelessly in love with said man it did not detract from the idea of making yourself beautiful for him and seeing his eyes light up with, if not love, she'd settle for lust.

She was a realist and this relationship could work if only she could keep her damned tongue under control. Luckily the few times her feelings had got the better of her and she'd blurted out her true feelings for him he hadn't noticed, but she couldn't rely on her luck holding out. She had to keep her mouth shut.

'Where did you have in mind?' She held the dress out at arm's length, admiring the way the hand-sewn beadwork caught the light. It was beautiful, but awfully dressy for the local places she knew of.

'Edinburgh…actually just outside.'

Her jaw dropped. 'Edinburgh!'

'The Dornie.'

'Dornie!' Izzy was neither star-struck or a

foodie, but everybody knew about the restaurant that had been opened the previous year. You needed to know someone just to get on the waiting list! It was apparently the place to be seen and she was assuming the food wasn't bad either.

'I have a jet on standby; we will be home before the witching hour if you wish. Do not look at me like this is everyday stuff for fairy godmothers.'

And billionaire playboys, except she had been forced to rethink many of her assumptions about him over the past few weeks, including the playboy reputation she had believed him to have. Izzy gave a wistful glance at the dress. 'Really?' The prospect of wearing something feminine was incredibly tempting.

'Would I lie to you?'

Izzy's smile faded. 'No,' she said slowly. 'I don't think you would.'

When had that happened?

She trusted him, which was no reason to cry, she thought, blinking back the hot tears she felt swimming in her eyes. She looked down and sniffed and when she lifted her head her blue eyes were guarded. It was just as well he hadn't been there when she had realised she had fallen in love with him.

That had been the day she had discovered her old sketchbook and had seen his face drawn on every page. It had hit her almost immediately that each likeness of him she had sketched had been drawn with love. Her sketchbook was a love story—an unrequited-love story. She had cried over the pages until they were soggy. She'd experienced love at first sight and she hadn't even known it!

'What time do we leave?'

There was a slight pause and when he replied she had the impression he had been on the brink of saying something else.

'Six-thirty…?'

Her mouth opened in a silent O of protest. 'I'll never manage that. Lily needs—'

'I will see to Lily. You go get ready.'

Tipping her head in acknowledgement of this suggestion she turned to leave, then, with her hand on the door handle, turned back. 'It's a lovely birthday present, thank you, Roman.'

'It is not your birthday present.' He watched her eyes flicker wider, saw the question in them and smiled. 'I hope the dress fits.'

It did fit.

It couldn't have fitted better and, nibbling her full lower lip, Izzy viewed her reflection through narrowed eyes from several angles.

It was perfect. The only thing she would have changed were the freckles on the swell of her bust where the square-cut neckline of the bodice was not as modest as it had appeared. But the rest, she gave a little nod of approval. Below knee length the beaded panels of the drop-waisted skirt swirled outwards when she moved, falling against her legs with a sexy swish.

The question was would Roman be as impressed?

The jury was still out on that one. She walked into the room a little while later complete with a jewelled, flapper-style headband placed in her glossy chestnut hair, her figure elongated by a pair of elegant spiky heels. Roman simply stared at her for what felt like a century, then tilted his head and said, 'You look good.'

It was hard not to feel deflated by such an underwhelming reaction, but then she had a tendency to expect too much when it came to their relationship.

Izzy felt impatient with herself. *Maybe,* she reflected grimly, *I ought to write 'He doesn't love you' a hundred times, then it might sink in.* Then she might stop laying herself open to this sort of disappointment.

When she had walked into the room Roman's vision had blurred. It had taken all his control not to grab her and take her right there. Ironic it had taken him some time to persuade her to wear the thing and now all he wanted to do was rip it off!

He had stood there like a statue struggling to control his rampant arousal, knowing that he couldn't even move without revealing his condition. His libido-whacked brain hadn't even been able to come up with something to cover up his lapse—he must have looked like a total idiot.

He wanted to cringe every time he thought about it.

But why?

Expressing his desire for Izzy had never been a problem for him, and definitely not an embarrassment! But this wasn't just desire, it was... He shook his head, refusing to acknowledge the word hovering there just on the outer limits of his consciousness, telling himself instead that she was just getting under his skin. On the other hand she was the mother of his child and it was only natural that there was a degree of emotional attachment. It didn't mean...

Bringing this internal debate to an end with a muttered curse, he shook his head and walked across the room, filling a heavy leaded crystal glass with brandy and lifting it to his lips.

It meant nothing, he told himself, draining the glass.

CHAPTER ELEVEN

'I THINK I could get used to this,' Izzy admitted as they disembarked from the private jet and into the waiting limousine. She repressed the urge to pinch herself. It felt as though she were playing a part in a film, but this was real.

'I think people might think I'm someone important,' she confided as he slid into the seat beside her.

'You are someone important.'

Her heart started thudding. 'I am?'

'You're the mother of our child.'

She hid her disappointment behind a smile of dazzling brilliance. While she was proud of being Lily's mother, she would have liked to be important for herself, not because she was part of a package deal.

'You owe me.'

If her film had been a romantic comedy he would have said, 'because you are the woman I love,' but this wasn't a romantic comedy or even a film.

It was her life and by most people's standards it was pretty amazing, so she told herself to stop whining and enjoy.

'I owe you?'

'The first person to mention the subject.' Baby talk by mutual agreement had been banned for the evening. 'And that was you.'

He lifted a concessionary finger and looked amused as he leaned back in his seat. Slipping the button on his dinner jacket, he shrugged and held up his hands in mock surrender. 'All right, you win.'

'So go on, give it up.' She held out her hand. 'What's my prize?'

Roman took her hand and placed it behind his neck. Leaning in close, he positioned his mouth over hers, catching her eyes with his as he whispered throatily, 'This.'

Her eyes closed as he kissed her with small

tantalising, nipping kisses that tugged at her lip, touched the corner of her mouth before going deeper. His arms were like steel bands wrapped around her, drawing her closer as he kissed her with a passion that amounted to desperation, kissed her as though he would drain her life force.

When his head lifted they were both breathing hard. They stayed close, his nose pressed to the side of hers, his fingers curled around her chin, stroking down the curve of her cheek.

'Was that my birthday present?'

'Pay attention, *cara*. That was your prize. This,' he added, leaning back in his seat to search the pocket of his jacket, 'is your present.'

Izzy looked at the small velvet box he held in his hand. 'I don't wear jewellery.'

'I'd noticed. I'll admit it does make present buying more difficult.' Though in his opinion her perfect satin-soft skin needed no adornment. He felt the familiar heat flicker in his belly as his eyes slid down the smooth column of her marble-pale neck and down to the freckle-sprinkled slopes of her breasts.

The flicker became a flame.

'So it's not jewellery?'

'Open it and see,' he urged, frowning at her apparent reluctance. He had taken a lot of trouble planning this moment, but her reaction was the one thing he wasn't able to plan or, as it turned out, predict.

She took a deep breath and opened the box, her normally animated voice sounding oddly flat to his ears as she said, 'It's beautiful.'

Beautiful hardly did the ring justice. The central diamond was massive and surrounded by dozens of smaller gems arranged like petals around the glittering centrepiece.

Frustrated, he compared her almost childlike enthusiasm for the dress with the stiff formality of her forced smile.

'You expected something else?' He placed his thumb under her small round chin and tilted her face up to him. 'You don't like diamonds?'

'Diamonds are… Is this an engagement ring?'

She had to be the only woman in the world who would need to ask. 'That was the idea. You do not have to sit on your hand. I will not force it on your finger.'

With a self-conscious flush she pulled her left hand free. 'But you said we wouldn't talk about—'

'Marriage,' he completed when she choked on the word. 'I agreed to wait and see if the trial was working, to see if we could work together as a unit, as a family.' Up until this moment he had thought they were a perfect fit, and not just in bed where she continued to delight and amaze him. 'I had thought that we were.' He arched a sardonic brow. 'You think differently?'

'No...not really,' she admitted slowly. 'But it's early days.'

Her addendum drew an incredulous look. 'How long did you have in mind?' he asked sardonically. 'Twenty years and then we will review the situation? I am sorry, Isabel, I have been very patient. These weeks have not been...unpleasant?' he bit out sarcastically.

Her reluctance felt like a betrayal. Their relationship had always been about Lily, about being with her, but he did not just look forward to seeing his daughter at the end of a day. He looked forward to seeing Isabel and spending time with her too. The sex between them was sensational and he had assumed they were on the same page here. But her lukewarm reaction had felt like a slap in the face... Actually the blow landed somewhat lower. It wasn't as though he had expected her to clap her hands and jump up and down with enthusiasm—well, actually, yes, he had.

Her lashes swept downwards. 'No, you know they haven't been unpleasant. Of course they haven't.'

He gave a shrug and waited.

'Can't we just leave things as they are?' The expression on his taut face made her stop and swallow before continuing in a fake cheery voice. 'I mean, like they say, if it's not broke don't fix it,' she quoted.

'I do not give a damn what *they say*,' he ground out. 'It may come as something of a surprise to you, but there are some women who would not consider it such a terrible thing to be married to me.'

'Well, marry them, then—all of them, for all I care!' she flung back.

'They are not the mother of my child.'

No, and that encapsulated the problem. The only reason he wanted to marry her was for Lily. Was it so wrong of her to want more?

Wrong maybe, unrealistic definitely. *You're not going to get more, Izzy,* said the voice of practicality in her head. *You take what's on offer or walk away from the table.*

The stark choice made her shiver. Over the past few weeks she had experienced the sort of life she had never even known existed. It wasn't just the incredible sex—though the thought of never losing herself in the sheer joy and bliss of belonging to him made her grow cold. No, it was so many other things too. Just hearing his voice, watching his face as he watched Lily, his dry sense of humour.

It was all about love.

She took a deep breath and thought it was worth a try.

'You're not going to pretend you're in love with me?'

She lowered her lashes in a defensive sweep; his silence spoke volumes and Izzy was lanced with an intense pain.

'I love Lily.'

She nodded. 'I know.' Watching Roman fall under the spell of his little daughter had been like watching a tender love story unfold, one that on occasions had brought emotional tears to her eyes. She squared her slender shoulders and lifted her head.

'Are you asking me to say I love you, Izzy? Is that what you're asking? Because I've already told you that—'

Pride made her keep her eyes trained on his face and not reveal by as much as a flicker how much his comment had mortified her. 'You don't do love. Yes, I know.' Izzy even managed a credible laugh as she hid the pain in her heart behind a practical façade.

'Relax, Roman, people say things in the heat of the...' Her eyes dropped as memories of the occasions when she had been unable to totally keep her feelings inside caused her rigid composure to slip.

'In bed,' he supplied bluntly.

'Let's leave bed out of one discussion.'

'It's the one place we have no discord.'

'You can't live in bed!' Struggling for composure, she lowered her voice to a dull monotone, adding woodenly, 'I know that you don't believe you'll ever—but what if you do fall in love with someone else, Roman? What happens then?' She thought that she could just about cope with the pain of loving him and knowing her love would never be returned, simply because she knew the pain of not being with him would be so much worse. But could she really bear to witness him falling in love with another woman and all the time wishing and wanting it to be her?

'It will not happen.'

His quiet certainty made her want to scream. 'All right then, if I fall in love.' She pulled back in her seat, shocked by the expression of black fury that surfaced in his eyes.

'I will make sure you don't.'

She did not read too much into that statement; she had challenged his male ego, that was all. She was his property.

'I know you think you can do anything.' And most of the time he was right. 'But you can't stop falling in love with someone.' *Ask the expert,* she thought dully. 'It just happens.'

'*Happens?* Things do not happen unless we allow them to and you will be too busy juggling the demands of our children with your work and—' He broke off mid-sentence, frowning fiercely and muttering something in his native tongue under his breath.

'Wait a moment.' The screen separating them from the driver swished silently down. 'Why are we stopped?' Roman rapped, realising that they were no longer moving, though he had no idea of how long they had been stationary.

The driver replied with a slightly embarrassed, 'We're here, sir.'

'We're not ready yet. Just keep on driving.'

'Yes, sir.'

Was he going to carry on driving round and round until she said yes?

'What is so funny?'

'You…me…us, I suppose. You said children?'

'Well, we managed it once and we weren't even trying. I see no reason why we shouldn't try again.' The sardonic humour in his voice was edged out by a harder tone as he admitted, 'I do not like to think of Lily as a lonely only child. So, yes, not immediately but—'

'Were you lonely?'

'Isabel, do not change the subject. Will you marry me?'

'You're the one who changes the subject every time I ask you anything about yourself.'

'I have told you more about myself than any other person on the planet.' He took her calf and pulled her foot into his lap. 'Very pretty,' he admitted, turning her foot to admire the thin-strapped high heels she wore. His fingers slid upwards over the curve of her calf. He felt the shiver that rippled through her body and smiled. 'You have a tendency to think too much about the past.'

'Better than ignoring it.' She broke off, closing her eyes and gasping as his fingers slid higher under the skirt of her dress. The rush of moist heat to the juncture of her thighs was instantaneous.

'Please, Roman, we're not alone...' she appealed, flashing a warning look towards the driver.

He flashed a predatory grin and withdrew his hand with a show of reluctance, but kept her foot in his lap. 'You like rules and conformity. I'd have said that marriage and you are a match made in heaven.'

'Are you saying I'm boring?' Helpless to evade his unblinking black stare, she dodged the question. 'I never saw myself married.'

'I never thought of myself as a father. Marriage will be a legal contract, nothing more. It will formalise what we have.'

'What do we have?' *Say love,* she willed him. *Say love.*

'We have Lily and the desire to make a home for her. We would not be going into this with any unrealistic expectations—that has to put us ahead of the game.'

For unrealistic expectations, she read love. The logic behind the confident pronouncement passed her by, but she was fully occupied in trying to fight the sudden desire to burst into tears.

'We will make it work for us because it's the best thing for Lily. You know it and I know it. Yes or no, Isabel?' He looked at her steadily, his normally expressive voice flat almost. The rigidity of his expression and the faint hint of colour along the sharp edge of his chiselled cheekbones were the only outward indication of the tension within.

Izzy sucked in a deep breath. Roman was not the shallow womaniser she had initially taken him for and he was a good father. He loved Lily—wasn't that enough? Ignoring the voice in her head that told her she was settling.

Yes, she was settling. She would never have a place in Roman's heart, but she could have a place in his life. They would be together, a family; it would be enough, she told herself. It would have to be, warned the voice in her head.

'Yes, I will marry you.'

For a moment his expression was unguarded. Then a moment later the blaze of male triumph was concealed by the dark mesh of his lashes.

Izzy felt a stirring of unease. He had got what he wanted, but for how long? What chance did such a one-sided marriage have? Pushing away the voice of doubt, she took the ring from its velvet bed and slid it onto her finger. 'It's very beautiful,' she said, holding out her hand for him to examine. She would have to have enough love for both of them.

'It's too big.' He had wanted it to be perfect.

'Not really…' The ring slipped around her finger and she shrugged. 'Well, maybe a little,' she conceded.

'We can get it adjusted. What are you doing?' he asked as she slipped it off.

The sharpness in his voice brought her head up. 'I can't wear it, Roman. I'll lose it.'

'You won't lose it.' He took her hand and pushed the ring back down her finger. 'It looks good on you,' he said, retaining the grip on her hand. Her fingers curled of their own volition around his.

Izzy felt her cheeks heat and her breathing quicken as their glances tangled and locked. The sexual tension that materialised from nowhere was so dense it had a texture and a taste of its own. Her eyelids felt heavy and her body, conditioned to respond to him, ached.

She swallowed and whispered an agonised. 'Oh, God!'

His dark, hawkish gaze riveted on Izzy's face and Roman expelled a long hissing sigh. 'Just hold that thought for later. In the meantime...' He gave a regretful sigh and, releasing her hand, leaned back in the seat.

'In the meantime?' she prompted.

'Are you hungry?' He saw her expression and gave a rumble of laughter. 'In a three-star Michelin sort of hungry?'

'I knew that…and, yes, I am.'

He dragged a hand across his face and wrenched his eyes off the pouting invitation of her luscious lips. 'Then let's go see if this place lives up to its reputation.'

The meal was, if anything, too much of a success and a bubbling Izzy spent the entire journey back babbling about the famous faces she'd spotted there.

'Why didn't you tell me you were friendly with Rob Fullwood? He's not as tall as he looks in films, but very good-looking. I think it's the eyes. Thank you, Gennaro,' she added, smiling at the burly Italian as he held the door wide for her to exit the four-wheel drive. She waited for Roman to walk around the car to meet her.

Roman gritted his teeth and glanced at his watch. He hoped this star-struck Izzy would vanish as quickly as she had appeared. One of the things he liked about Izzy was that, unlike many women, she did not feel the need to fill every silence with words.

'I am not friendly with him. We have met, that is all.'

'You have more than met his girlfriend.'

The words she had been trying so hard not to say just slipped out, and there they were, impossible to take back.

Izzy veiled her gaze and began to walk quickly towards the front door. 'I hope Lily has been good for Chloe.'

Halfway up the steps Roman caught her up. He caught her arm and pulled her back to face him.

Izzy stared at her hand, twisting the ring around her finger as she gave a theatrical shiver. 'Goodness, it's quite cold, isn't it?'

'No. Is that why you've been so weird?'

Her head came up. 'Is what why…? I have not been weird.'

He arched a sardonic brow. 'Yes, I have slept with Connie Brady.'

She felt the stab of jealousy like a sword thrust. 'That's really none of my business.'

'You don't have to be jealous. We only lasted a week.'

'I only lasted a night,' she countered spikily.

'The two situations are not comparable.'

An image of the tall Nordic blonde model with the endless legs, hair extensions and false eyelashes came into her head. Most men had been intrigued by her, particularly her gravity-defying breasts. 'True, I have a baby and she has massive boobs!'

She was not aware that she was clutching her own boobs when his amused glance lingered there. She dropped her hands hastily and reminded herself of the old adage of quality being superior to quantity.

'You are jealous!'

Izzy narrowed her eyes and delivered a haughty look. 'I don't much like the idea of walking into a room filled with your ex-lovers and having them laugh about me behind my back. Don't…' she snapped as he laid his hands on her shoulders.

He ignored her.

'I think the chances of you being in a room filled with my exes is unlikely, but, that aside, they will not be laughing at you when you are my wife. They will be envying you.'

A bubble of laughter emerged from her aching throat. 'Do you know how arrogant that sounds?'

'Yes, but it made you laugh so who cares?' He hooked a thumb under her chin and turned her face up to him. 'While the women will be envying you the men will be envying me. You put all those women in the shade tonight.' His glance slid down the slender length of her shapely body. 'I have wanted to kiss you all night and all you have done is witter on like a star-struck teenager. *Madre di Dio!*'

'What?'

'I have just realised that one day Lily will be a teenager.'

His horrified expression drew another laugh from Izzy.

'But seriously, Isabel, you do not have to be jealous. I have had lovers in the past, but once we are married I will respect my vows.'

Izzy nodded and expelled a sigh, allowing the

jealous poison to drain away with the trapped air... A tiny portion lingered stubbornly.

She was ready to believe that the casual lovers he had had over the years meant nothing, but Roman had been engaged once before to Lauren. Lauren, the beautiful blonde who had dumped him. Theirs had not been a casual relationship; he had been going to marry her, not for practical reasons, but for love.

She touched the ring on her finger and looked up at him and felt something twist hard in her chest. He was so beautiful. She had ruined the entire evening by being eaten up with jealousy, but there was still some evening to enjoy.

'That kiss you were talking about...?'

She shivered as he framed her face between his big hands. The kiss was deep with a passion that sent a shiver of pleasure through her body and without a word he picked her up.

In the bedroom they stood facing each other and in the moonlight they undressed slowly, punctuating the slow striptease with murmurs and moans of pleasure and deep, languid, drowning kisses that made Izzy's lips tingle and her insides melt.

She closed her eyes as he removed the last item of her clothing, her panties, pressing a kiss to the curls at the juncture of her thighs as she stepped out of them.

Kneeling, he curved his hands around the taut curve of her rounded bottom, kissing his way up her belly. He stood up, slowly running his hands up her body to cup and caress the creamy swells of her aching breasts.

As he kissed her breasts, running his tongue across the engorged rosy peaks, Izzy's fingers closed over the hot, silky shaft of his erection, drawing a raw groan from his throat.

They both stumbled to the bed, falling on it in a tangle of limbs.

His hands shook as he parted her legs, but Izzy was shaking too hard herself to notice. The mixture of raw passion and tenderness in his face brought tears to her eyes in response to emotions she had no words to express.

A keening cry was wrenched from her dry

throat as he slid fully into her, burying himself. The primal connection was stronger than she had ever felt it before as they moved together, straining towards the final explosion of mind-numbing pleasure.

When Roman finally rolled off her, she was relaxed in every cell of her body and she curled up against him and fell asleep.

Surely he could not make love like that without loving her a little, was her last wistful thought.

The next day Roman left early to attend a charity auction he had committed to months earlier.

'I would get out of it if I could,' he said, sitting on the bed to kiss her goodbye. A few minutes later he was back.

Izzy looked up at him drowsily. 'What's wrong?'

'Come with me.'

She blinked, startled. 'You mean to the charity auction?'

He nodded. 'Why not? I can wait.'

Fully awake now, Izzy gave a twisted smile.

'I'd love to, but I've already arranged to go shopping to the paint wholesaler's and Chloe is coming with me. She's a great sounding board and we're dropping Lily off for a play date with—'

'Fine. It was just a thought.'

She thought she saw something in his face that suggested her response had not pleased him, but when she had rubbed her bleary eyes it was not there… Maybe she had imagined it.

'Enjoy your day and I hope Lily enjoys her play date.'

Lily didn't, as it turned out, as she was a bit out of sorts when she woke that morning. Izzy cancelled her play date and her trip to the wholesaler's.

By lunchtime Lily's out of sorts had become something a lot more worrying. Lily was crying inconsolably, thrashing around in her cot redfaced. Izzy took her temperature and the reading on the strip was so high that she took it again.

The reading was a degree higher.

Should she bundle Lily in the car and drive to the local emergency department or should she ring for an ambulance? Having been in the habit of making decisions for herself for most of her life, it struck her forcibly how much her mindset had changed when she found herself wishing that Roman were here to share the responsibility with.

After a few minutes she no longer cared if she came across as an overanxious mother and dialled the emergency number.

Rocking Lily in her arms, as the baby had gone scarily quiet, she tried to ring Roman, but kept getting put straight through to his messaging service. She decided not to leave an alarming message for him when there was a chance this was a false alarm and took the decision to wait until she could speak directly to him.

There were several times during the ambulance journey that she regretted this decision and would have given anything to know that Roman was on his way or even waiting for her at the hospital.

The doctors in the accident department were attentive and quietly efficient, which was comforting; what they had to say was not.

'It looks very much like Lily has appendicitis. We need to operate.'

'But she's a baby… No, that can't be right.' Fear tightened like an icy stone in her chest, panic clawing its way into her brain. She struggled to keep it at bay.

She had to stay in control; Lily needed her. She made herself take a deep breath and tried to lower her tension-hunched shoulders… *I want Roman… no, I can do this myself.*

'I realise this is alarming, but we will look after Lily for you and—'

'Of course, I'm sorry… When will you…?'

'Immediately.'

Lily's dark lashes fluttered against her cheeks and her eyes were filled with fear as she stared at the medic. 'That's not good, is it?'

'If you could sign the consent for us?'

Izzy sniffed and wiped a shaky hand across her face. 'Of course, she's just so little and…of course.'

Her hand continued to shake so hard she doubted her signature was legible. Everything happened very quickly and Izzy still wasn't sure whether to read good or bad things into this, but one minute she was sitting next to Lily's cot and the next she was walking along a seemingly endless corridor beside a cheery porter who wheeled Lily's cot to the entrance of the operating theatre.

Everyone was very kind but when she had to say goodbye to Lily she couldn't hold back the tears, as much as she tried. Back on the ward they promised that they would let her know the moment Lily was out of surgery and offered her a cup of tea.

Unable to stomach the idea of swallowing anything, she refused. Pacing the small cubicle, she dialled Roman. On the fourth time the phone was picked up.

She felt weak with relief until a voice she did not recognise said, 'This is Roman Petrelli's phone.'

A female voice.

'Who is this?'

There was a pause the other end, then a small laugh.

'Who is this? I want to speak to Roman.'

'Don't we all, darling?' the female voiced drawled.

Before she could respond Izzy heard a very familiar voice in the background. She didn't catch all of what Roman said; actually just one word—Lauren.

It was enough.

'Am I speaking to Lauren St James?'

'Yes, Roman is here now—'

'It doesn't matter—you can give him a message.'

'Sure, but—'

'Tell him his daughter is in surgery and that he can go to hell and stay there and I never want to hear, speak to or see him again!'

Having delivered her message, she sat on the plastic chair wanting to cry, but there were no tears. She felt cold and empty inside.

She hated him.

Later Roman had no memory of the drive from the city to the hospital; he just knew he made it in record time.

When he saw her face he immediately thought the worst.

His eyes went to the empty cot and Roman felt as though someone had reached into his chest and ripped out a vital organ. His lovely little girl... He couldn't bear life without his daughter, either of the women in his life—they were his heart. His haunted glance slid to Isabel. How had he been so stupid?

He had let himself love Lily, but he had been too weak and too scared to allow himself to admit that his heart held two women—mother and daughter, the two for ever inextricably linked.

And now one was gone...his baby. He breathed through the pain—his pain could wait. Right now Isabel needed him.

She looked like a broken doll, so pale and fragile, so vulnerable. It was enough to rouse the protective instincts of even a hardened professional.

But he was not a professional; he was the man who loved her. The man who had spent the last weeks avoiding facing this knowledge because basically he was a coward, he concluded contemptuously. A woman had rejected him once, a shallow woman who had little to recommend her but a pretty face and a family tree that stretched back into the mists of time, and for that reason he had decided to exclude the possibility of love from his life with all the logic and self-preservation instincts of a wounded animal.

He'd not been licking his wounds, he'd been nursing his bruised ego.

'Isabel.' The blazing blue eyes that lifted to him were not tear-filled, they were hate-filled. *'Tesoro mio.'*

'Do not speak to me. Do not touch me!' she shrieked shrilly, glaring at his outstretched hand as though it were a striking snake. 'You are not wanted here.'

'Well, tough, because I am here.' He looked at the empty cot and swallowed again. His eyes misted as he thought of Lily, the ache in his chest so intense that it felt like a steel band tightening like a vice around his ribcage. 'I should have been here for you.' His hands tightened into white-knuckled fists at his sides as he asked in a pain-filled whisper. 'When she…did she suffer?'

Izzy was blind to his suffering. 'Of course she suffered. Her appendix was about to burst, they said.'

'Appendix…burst…' His relief was cautious, the relief of a man who had lost something precious and was being offered it back. If he was given this second chance he would not waste it. 'You mean she is not…our little Lily is alive.'

The break in his deep voice brought her eyes to his face where strain drew the skin tight across his perfect bones, deepening the lines that radiated from his mouth and fanned out from around his eyes. Izzy gripped her lip between her teeth and fought against a tide of empathy. This was not about shared pain—she was alone.

'She's in recovery now,' Izzy said, watching as the colour slowly seeped back into his face and the awful grey receded. 'You thought she was dead?' She hated him but not enough to wish that on him. She wound her hands together to stop herself reaching out for him.

He nodded and swallowed.

'I didn't say…'

'I got your message.' Lauren had taken some delight in relaying it word for word—not that Lauren had the power to hurt him. 'But when I saw you looking so…'

'Needy and pathetic?' she charged acidly.

'Broken, I jumped to the conclusion.'

Izzy had paled at the description that was so close to how she did feel. She felt as though she had been shattered into a thousand pieces.

'Well, you were wrong so you can go.' She stuck out her chin and added, 'We don't need you!' Then proceeded to spoil the effect by bursting into tears.

In a heartbeat he was at her side, drawing her into the protective circle of his arms. She stood there sobbing, her head against his heart, knowing all the time she felt warm and protected in his arms that it was a lie.

He stroked her hair. 'I know what you think but you're wrong.'

Izzy lifted her tear-stained face and tried to pull away.

'No, you will listen. You will not continue to torture yourself and me with your imaginings. Lauren and I were seated at the same table at the charity auction.'

'Just a coincidence, I suppose.'

'I would hardly plan to meet another woman and then invite you to the same event, would I? Think about it.'

Izzy did and the first chink of doubt appeared in her betrayal scenario.

'She had your phone…'

He grimaced as he recalled the sequence of events that had led to this. 'I left my phone on the table. You know how I am with my phone.'

She nodded warily. For an organised man Roman managed to lose his phone more times a day than she could count. She had teased him about it, especially as often it was right under his nose.

'I was not at the table when it rang. I was with Lauren's husband, being fleeced for raffle tickets.

I think it is likely I have won a balloon flight over the Masai Mara. How do you feel about balloon flights, *cara*?'

How do you feel about me?

'Lauren is married?'

He nodded.

Was it possible? A slow flush ran up under her skin until her face was burning.

'I blame myself. I knew you thought that I still had feelings for Lauren and I let you think it, because while you thought I was in love with her I wouldn't have to admit even to myself…*especially* to myself, that I had fallen in love with you.' He gave an uncomfortable shrug. 'I was so determined not to have my pride trampled over again that I refused to acknowledge what I was feeling. I was scared to admit that my fate, my happiness, depended on another human being— you. I let you think it was all about Lily, but it was always all about love.' He took her hand and raised it to his lips. 'You hold me in your hand, *cara*. I hope you will allow me into your heart.'

She stared at him in utter amazement, his smoky voice sending shivers down her spine.

'Roman, you've always been there. I think there was always an emptiness inside me that only you could fill.'

He kissed her then with a tenderness and passion that brought tears of emotion to her eyes.

He drew back a little and framed her face with one big hand. 'When I think of you all alone trying to cope with this… But of course you did cope alone—you are a remarkable woman and a perfect mother. I know you don't need me, *cara*, but will you have me? I know I have proposed before but this time is different.'

'I know,' she said, looking at him with eyes that were bright as stars. 'And I do need you. I have loved you so much and not being able to say it has been…hell!'

They kissed until the sound of a phone ringing in the main ward brought them back to earth.

Roman took her hand and pushed her into a chair, then dropped down into a squat at her side. Holding her hands between his, he said, 'Now tell me what happened and how our baby is. I wish so much that I had been there for you both. In the future I will always be there for you—you do know that.'

The anxiety and sincerity in his face brought a lump to her throat. 'Of course, you couldn't have known.'

'So tell me.'

She did and the sharing had a cleansing effect. She was finishing relating the tale and Roman was mopping her tears when the door opened and a cot was wheeled in.

'Here she is,' said the pretty nurse. 'Now, don't you worry about the drip—that's just until she starts taking fluids. Doctor will be along shortly but there are no problems. Everything is going to be fine.'

Izzy looked from her baby to her future husband and nodded. 'Yes, I do believe it is,' she said.

And even if it wasn't, she would always have Roman there to support her through the bad times and, of course, laugh with her through the good times.

'I wish I'd been here,' Roman said for the umpteenth time as he gazed into the cot.

Izzy went and took his hand. 'You're here now. That's what matters.'

She couldn't ask for anything more.

EPILOGUE

'AND it all began here,' Emma said with a sigh as she dropped to her knees to straighten the hem of Izzy's dress.

Izzy smiled and thought, *Actually, it all began in a crowded bar,* but she didn't correct her sister.

'It's so romantic and so quick too—three months.'

'No so quick,' Izzy murmured, glancing at her daughter, who looked as pretty as a picture in pink and was clutching a satin cushion in her chubby fingers.

'Watch your veil…' Michelle moved in to twitch the gauzy short antique lace that had belonged to her own grandmother. 'So pretty, darling,' Michelle said with a misty smile. 'You look truly glowing, and don't worry—I'll give Lily the ring at the very last minute.'

'Wing!' Lily said, her face wreathing in an expectant smile.

'Yes, darling…rings.' Izzy smiled. It had been decided that their daughter would deliver the wedding rings and the toddler had been given ample training in her role, though taking into account her tendency to try and eat the rings it had also been decided that she would be given the rings by Michelle at the crucial moment.

'Emma, remember—do not stoop when you go up the aisle.'

'Yes, Mum,' her willowy daughter responded to this maternal directive with a long-suffering sigh, adding as her mother vanished into the church with Lily, 'Do you know how many times a day she says that to me?'

She encountered Izzy's dreamy stare and grinned.

'You're not listening to a word I'm saying, are you?'

'No,' Izzy admitted. She wasn't nervous, she was just happy; she doubted people ever got to feel this happy.

Emma laughed. 'You look so soppy and I don't blame you. If I was going to get married to a hunk like Roman I would be on another planet too, but for goodness' sake don't cry,' she instructed firmly. 'Rachel looked terrible when her mascara ran. On half the photos she looks like a panda,' she continued with her usual exuberance. 'But you look much prettier than Rachel did,' she added loyally. 'A pity you didn't choose that big dress with the proper long train. Not,' she added quickly, 'that that doesn't look nice.'

'Thank you.' Izzy gave a serene smile and smoothed down the dress she had picked in preference to the elaborate creation her sister had considered the ultimate in romance. A simple strapless, ankle-length cream silk, it clung to her curves, revealing a suggestion of cleavage, emphasising her pert bottom and making her waist look tiny, managing to be both sexy and demure.

Izzy had fallen in love with it the moment she had seen it.

The same way she had fallen in love with her gorgeous husband the moment she had seen him.

And he had fallen in love with her. It still didn't seem real sometimes, but it was, and Izzy had contractual evidence. No one else knew they had already married at a civil ceremony a week after Lily had been discharged from hospital. It had just been the three of them with a cleaner and a passer-by as witnesses. Roman had said they had wasted long enough and he wasn't prepared to waste another second.

It had not been romantic like today, in a traditional way with the pretty village church decked in clouds of white gypsophila and red roses and the beautiful dress and the speeches to come, but for Izzy it had been the most perfect day of her life when Roman had stood there, this strong, proud man with the glint of tears in his beautiful eyes, and said he would love her for ever.

She didn't need the window dressing; she just needed the man she loved and their baby girl. Not that she didn't intend to enjoy every second of this day. There was no way she was going to rob her family, Michael in particular, of the wedding they craved, and his chance to walk his daughter up the aisle.

'Ready, darling?'

Izzy smiled at her father, who had been striding nervously up and down the path outside the church, and took the arm he proffered. 'I am.'

The only thing she remembered about the service afterwards was the laugh that had rippled through the church when Lily had stolen the show when she delivered the rings, and Roman's face when he had turned and looked at her.

The incandescent love and pride in his face had brought the tears she had vowed not to shed; thank heaven for waterproof mascara!

Falling into the wedding car later in a cloud of confetti, she sank back into the seat and waved through the window at the crowds of well-wishers. When the car drew off, she turned and found Roman watching her. Her tummy did the crazy flip lurch it always did when she saw him; he was so handsome, and especially today in his beautifully tailored morning suit.

'What are you looking at?'

'The most beautiful woman in the world…and you're mine…' He took her hand and raised it to his lips, still holding her eyes with his. 'My woman.'

His smoky voice sent delicious shivers down Izzy's spine.

'You know,' he mused, stroking her cheek with one brown finger, 'I will never get tired of saying that.'

She caught his wrist and pressed a kiss to his palm. 'And I won't get tired of hearing it,' she promised, looking at him through the dark screen of her lashes.

Roman's free hand came up to cup her face. 'Your skin is so soft. You must remember to put on plenty of sun screen—apparently we are promised a very hot September.'

Izzy smiled. They were spending their honeymoon at Roman's villa at Lake Como.

'What is that secretive little cat's-got-the-cream smile for?' he wanted to know.

'I got you.'

Izzy broke away, breathless from the passionate kiss, some time later as the car arrived at the hotel where the reception was being held.

'Ready?' he asked, watching with a smile as she desperately tried to straighten her veil.

Ready for the rest of my life with you, Izzy thought, and nodded. At the last moment before they emerged into the September sunshine and their waiting guests, she caught his wrist.

'Is something wrong, *cara*?' Roman asked, picking up on her tension.

'Not wrong,' she admitted. 'Pretty right, actually. I didn't mean to tell you now, but...'

'The tension is killing me here, *cara*.'

'You know that appointment you planned to make to check that Lily was not a one-off—that you can... Well, don't bother, because it looks like you can.'

'You mean...?' Roman swallowed, his eyes going to her trim middle. 'You are...'

She nodded. 'I did the test last night.' The night Michelle had insisted she didn't spend with the groom. 'It's been killing me not telling you. I wanted to blurt it out right there in the church. You're happy?'

'Happy!' he exclaimed, pulling her into his arms. 'I am the luckiest man in the world!'

The ripple of applause and laughter given by the waiting guests caused Izzy to draw back, pressing her hand against his breastbone to lever herself off his lean body.

'Roman, people are watching.'

'Shall I tell them to go away?'

'Roman, you can't tell guests to go away.'

His wicked grin flashed. 'Watch me,' he said. Izzy did.

* * * * *